The Rising Prince

MAFIA EMPIRE
BOOK ONE

SIMONE FOX

CRAVE
PUBLISHING

The Rising Prince

First Print Edition: May 2023

Crave Publishing

Kailua, HI 96734

www.cravepublishing.net

Formatting: Crave Publishing

ISBN-13: 978-1-64034-668-0

Reading Order

PART ONE

"The Rising Prince" story starts here...
↓
A Billionaire's Secrets Series
By Simone Fox

Lured (Book #1)
An Arranged Marriage Romance

Provoked (Book #2)
A Mafia Romantic Suspense

Reading Order

PART TWO

Enjoy these other great reads that take place in the same world as The Rising Prince...

Deep Dark Secrets Series
By J.J. Love and Simone Fox

Instant Billionaire (Book #1)
"I was a fan of weddings, until I was forced into one with one of the most despicable human beings I've ever met..."

Instant Heiress (Book #2)
"I'm the rightful heiress to our family throne and someone is trying to take it from me..."

Prologue

MAX

I HAD TO SAY, sitting alone in a bar in downtown Brooklyn on a Friday night wasn't my idea of a fun time.

What I'd expected when coming here and what I was currently getting were on opposite sides of the spectrum, and it was starting to make me feel fucking antsy.

This bar was in a shady spot down in the underbelly of Brooklyn, snuck between two finance buildings that ran along the long alleyway that opened up into a small hub where drugs, guns, and all the riff-raff liked to hang out.

Normally, I liked going to bars with a little bit more class, but I'd had a hard day, so blowing off steam with a pretty girl's wet mouth all over me wouldn't be hard to find even in this kind of place.

Tossing another few dollars onto the bar, I caught the attention of the man behind it and held up two fingers to him. He nodded to me and headed to the other side of the bar, grabbing me a fresh glass off the top rack to fill.

This little project I had going on with Ricard was starting to really become a hassle more than it was supposed to be. I'd begun it because I'd been bored walking the halls of the Machiavelli family estate with fuck-all to do and way too much pent-up energy that was going to start getting me into trouble if I wasn't careful enough.

When Ricard had come to me with a proposition to start some kind of side business behind his parents' backs, I had a hard time saying no. I mean, what kind of influence would I be not to let the kid spread his wings when his own father clearly wasn't going to encourage it? In fact, the old man was recently going so far as to clip his damn wings before he could even make it out of the nest.

That kind of shit pissed me off to no end.

Not like it was triggering any of my age-old daddy issues or anything.

Not at all.

Once the bartender slid my drink down to me, I grabbed it and chugged back half of it. Dredging up that kind of shit wasn't going to do anyone a favor—least of all me.

Better to forget and move on.

Across the way, and at the other end of the bar, I

watched as a woman made her way over to one of the bar stools tucking into the very corner.

She simultaneously looked completely out of place but then not—with the way she looked. She was wearing a light t-shirt and a leather jacket over it, some patches of it roughed up around the collar and arms that made it seem like she'd done her fair share of street fighting.

What stood out about her was her face. She was too beautiful to be in a dump like this—let alone by herself from the looks of it.

She had long, thick, black hair that had tight waves to it, framing around her dark, tan skin that the yellow light shining over her didn't serve any justice for her. Her dark eyes scanned around the bar, stopping right as they landed on me.

That perfectly plush mouth of hers—the kind that would look good wrapped around a hard cock—smiled.

I smiled back.

Look, I was a simple creature. I saw something I liked, I wasn't afraid to go get it. That was the difference between Caleb and me. While he was fine with brooding in the shadows, I liked to get out and live a little.

Especially since my life expectancy was putting me at middle age at the moment.

Getting up from my stool, I took my glass with me and headed over to her side. Her eyes tracked me as I moved, carefully taking me in the closer I got to her.

She rested her cheek on her hand, those long lashes of hers fanning over her eyes a few times.

"Hey," I said, taking the stool next to hers. "What're you drinking?"

That smile widened. "Surprise me."

Oh, I liked her already.

"You adventurous?" I asked.

"Of course."

Excellent. My kind of woman.

Waving the bartender back over to us, I ordered two more drinks and then downed the rest of mine before sliding the empty glass back over.

"So, what's a pretty girl like you doing in a place like this?"

She laughed softly. "Came here for a drink." Her eyes darted up and down me again. "And maybe a little company."

I leaned forward. "Well, it looks like you came to the right place."

We didn't even get through the door to my hotel room before I was shoving her up against the wall. I supposed this was probably a sign I should've gotten laid way sooner than this. My pent-up frustration of being benched now that Caleb was gone off doing whatever that prick Liam had assigned him over in New York.

I'd always had a comfortable amount of attachment to the man, and now that he was over three thousand miles away, it kind of soured my day more of the time.

Hence the getting involved with Ricard scheme.

See, I hadn't exactly told Caleb any of this because I knew he'd one, disapprove, and two, tell me to stop before I got in over my head.

Which I supposed was a fair judgment, considering I tended to do things before thinking it all the way through. However, I was also a scrappy kind of guy, so things typically tended to work out in my favor.

All of this was well and good except for the fact that none of Ricard's options had panned out so far. How the fuck was I supposed to help him jumpstart his empire off the ground with nothing to fan the burning coals underneath him if I had no fire to start it in the first place?

He carried his father's name, of course, but we were also doing this behind his back, so using that to our advantage was out of the question.

Hence the pent-up frustration.

A hand tugged hard on the back of my hair, separating my lips from hers.

"Pay attention. I didn't let you bring me back here to give me the bare minimum."

A zing of thrill rushed through me.

Oh, I kind of liked a woman who could tell me what she wanted.

That was fun.

Grinning, my hand came around to right under

her ass, where I smacked one of her cheeks hard over her tight pants. She let out a surprised gasp, tightening her hand in my hair.

"Maybe I should put you on your knees so you can be taught manners," she said.

Fuck, am I into this?

"Aw, don't be like that."

She shoved me away from her, causing me to stumble back farther into my hotel room. I was already panting like a dog, and this little interaction was making me practically want to beg like one too.

Funny how little it took to get me off.

Another reason why I needed to get laid more often.

I walked backward away from her, smiling as I went. I'd give her the choice if she wanted to follow me or not; I wasn't going to force her under me if she was turned off already by me getting lost in my thoughts.

It wasn't that I wasn't into all of this. It was sex, and I'd be stupid not to be turned on by a woman as hot as her.

Unfortunately, since leaving Las Vegas, my head seemed to always be swimming with schemes and plans and whatever else took up space while I navigated these foreign waters.

"There you go," she said, coming over to me and cupping my cheeks between her hand. "Drifting off again."

I smirked. "Maybe I need to be taught how to pay attention. I've always been bad at that lately."

Something in her eyes flared at my words. Almost like she was considering taking up the challenge or not. Finally, when she let go of me, she stepped back.

"You know what?" she said. "Turn around."

Raising my brow, I slowly turned until my back was facing her. "Is this the part where you pull a knife on me and demand all my cash?"

She laughed. "I doubt you have enough to actually be worth the trouble."

Wow, ouch.

"I look that rough, huh?" I drawled.

When she grabbed one of my wrists, she yanked it back behind me. Something metal wrapped around it, and then she grabbed at the other.

"Whoa, whoa." I danced out of her hold. "What's this?"

"I like you better when you aren't talking."

"Wha—?" I didn't have time to ask what the fuck *that* meant before she was grabbing a hold of the front of my shirt and yanking me down just far enough for her to shove something cotton tasting into my mouth.

The fuck?

Taking the stunned moment, she grabbed my other wrist to spin me back around, handcuffing me completely.

Looking at her over my shoulder, she stepped back to survey her work. "Hmm, I think this will do nicely."

Damn, leave it to me to bring home a dominatrix.

Oh, well. Hopefully she knew what she was doing

because I really didn't feel like spending all night trying to bust out of these cuffs after she robbed me.

To my surprise, though, she shoved me back onto the bed, trapping my arms under me. The angle was uncomfortable but not horrible. It at least gave me enough room to shimmy back onto the bed to keep from falling on my ass.

The woman slowly peeled off her layers, tossing them one by one onto the floor until she was in a matching lacy set of lingerie.

Ah, I see. So this was very much planned.

Honestly, as bad as it sounded, I was kind of honored that she chose me to roll around in the sheets with. Not that I was a bad-looking dude or anything, despite the face scar.

When she got closer to me, she wasted no time in popping the front button on my pants and then pulling them apart. I was hard as fuck already, and this little charade we were doing was making it bad enough that my balls were starting to hurt.

She grabbed either side of the waist band, pulling it down just enough to pop me free.

"Well, I'm glad you were hiding this surprise from me," she said, wrapping her hand around my cock.

Her fingers were delicate looking as she moved them up and down a few times—something that I wasn't expecting given her personality. There were distinct callouses, though, which interested me more.

How did such a beautiful woman get *those*?

Tilting my head back, I let her touch me. It felt

fucking good, especially since she was clearly skilled in this area.

It wasn't long before she was crawling up onto the bed to straddle me, her fingers hooked around her panties to pull them to the side. My teeth sank into whatever it was she'd shoved into my mouth, biting back a moan as she slid down onto me.

Fuuuuuuck.

"Mmmm." She rolled her hips a few times, getting a nice steady rhythm going before she began to ride me.

Holy fuck, did I score or what?

My shoulders were cramping from my arms being pinned under me for so long, my fingers already going numb with pins and needles now that I had not only my body weight, but hers as well when she placed her hands on my chest and leaned into them.

Fuck, this was so hot, though, her using me like some kind of fuck toy.

I never knew I'd be into this, but here I was, praying that I didn't cum too soon and make all of this too early of a wrap-up with my balls throbbing like I'd never been touched before.

Her long hair was draped down her back, the curly ends bouncing with every roll of her hip. Too fucking bad I couldn't reach out and grab a good handful of it to yank it back like she did with mine. Give her a little taste of her own medicine.

Using as much of the angle as I could, my hips

bucked up into hers, my cock spearing deep enough into her that it had her gasped.

She slapped my chest with one of her hands. "No. Behave."

Fuck, if she kept talking to me like I was a fucking dog, I was actually going to cum.

"I didn't think you'd be this naughty being restrained like this." Her hand cupped my jaw again, her grip painfully tight. "I thought your mouth was going to be the biggest problem about you."

I wanted to laugh. That's fucking delightful that she thought that. Not only was I a loud mouth, but apparently I gave off the air as one too.

What I *didn't* find delightful was how she lifted up her hips completely until my cock slid right out of her and smacked down onto my belly.

What. The. Fuck.

She smirked. "See, now you get punished."

Her hips came back down to press against mine. Her pussy lips spread just enough to get my cock between them again while she rolled them over the length of me. It was barely enough to get me off and pissed me off way more than it should have.

When her head tilted back, she groaned.

With every pass of her hips on me, her breath hitched over and over. Clearly the head of my cock was rubbing right up against her clit, getting her off even when I wasn't. I watched her use me, her hands tightening around my face as her body shuddered and she finally came.

"Mmm…" Her eyes opened again. "I guess that'll do."

Excitement shot through me again. I couldn't wait to be inside her once more—

The woman let go of my face in order to swing her leg back around, getting off of me. As she finally got herself standing back up on the floor, she pulled her panties back over to cover herself.

Using my aching shoulders, I pushed until I was halfway sitting up.

There's no way she's going to leave me like this.

My cock was *throbbing*. My balls were so tight, they felt like they were about to explode.

She paid me absolutely no attention as she went about gathering her clothes again, putting them on layer by layer. When she was finally dressed—barely looking ruffled at all—she turned to nod at me.

"You got a handle on those, right?"

HUH?

I must have some kind of incredulous expression on my face, because it made her laugh.

"See ya."

I could barely breathe as she sauntered over to the door and left without another word. My door closed behind her with a heavy thud; no other sounds in the room, other than my own labored breathing, could be heard.

What the fuck was *that*?!

Growling, I rolled over so that I could better push myself up onto my feet. I was dizzy from being bent at such a weird angle that it took me a moment to recalibrate myself before heading over to my bag that I had tossed as an afterthought over by the closet.

Bending just enough to get down onto my knees again, I scooted over until my back was facing it. Luckily, I was pretty damn good at not only knowing the contents of my bag and where everything was, but also being able to using my hands backward.

After finally finding a lock pick, I got the cuffs off and tossed them away from me. Offensive things that didn't even get me off. What the fuck?

Taking the wad out of my mouth, I squinted at it. Looked like a fucking sock.

Nice. She got herself off, left me hanging, and probably used some old dirty sock to gag me.

And here I thought I was actually going to be having a good night.

Rolling my eyes at myself, I stood and then looked down at my still-hard cock. You know what, I didn't even want to look at it anymore. I was too pissed that I'd *actually* gotten used like a damn dildo with no added benefit of getting off myself. Wasn't that what dominatrices were supposed to be about? Getting their playthings off?

Somehow, this all seemed like one big punishment. But for what, I had no clue. I didn't think I offended her when I was at the bar.

Honestly, though, who fucking knew? I was too tired and annoyed to keep running through the situation until my brain exploded trying to figure out where the hell I went wrong.

Maybe she was just crazy.

Yeah, crazy hot, my very helpful brain supplied.

Shaking my head, I stripped right by the door and left my clothes tossed in a pile next to my bag. I needed to shower before I got going.

Ricard was probably waiting for me anyways.

CHAPTER 1

Max

Four Weeks Later...

THE FLIGHT in from Las Vegas hadn't been bad, just too long in my opinion.

While I could normally occupy myself with in-house movies and bad sitcoms, I had an unfortunate case of my head being far too full with plans for this upcoming meeting.

Ever since Caleb and Sam had taken off to flee the country, it'd just been me and Ricard doing what we were doing—making sure that our plan for domination was in full effect.

I hated lying to my best friend about the details when he'd asked—he had way more pressing things to be worrying about than me getting myself deeper involved with the mafia. I was sure he had a gut feeling about it; Caleb always had a sixth sense when it came to those sort of things.

This, though, was far outside his scope. How in the world could he predict that I'd be trying to build Ricard his own empire to rule over with myself tugging at the strings behind the scenes? It's just not something that anyone would think about, let alone guess.

I'd come up with the plan right after Caleb and Sam had left: with Liam out of the picture and his daughter gone with the wind to wherever it was she was hiding out, it gave Ricard prime opportunity to snatch up those contacts and make them his.

Liam's network was far wider reaching than probably any of us predicted. I was sure that the deeper we waded into these waters, the more shit we were going to dredge up. Some might not be in our favor, but those few contracts that we could poach and make ours would be invaluable.

"We ready?" Ricard asked me, straightening his tie once again.

"Yeah. You remember what we talked about?"

He nodded, his eyes focused on me with an intensity that I'd come to respect. "We're just here to introduce ourselves and make contact."

"Exactly. Don't be too pushy or they'll know something's up. Especially with Liam being gone. It hasn't been that long. I'm sure the news is still working its way through the grapevine."

Ricard nodded. "I'll keep that in mind. You'll be outside, though?"

"Yup. I'll be waiting to hear all the deets when you get back."

"Don't get into trouble."

I flashed him a smile. "No promises."

As our car pulled up to the front entrance to the Rosetti family's estate, I waited for our driver to come around and open my door before stepping out. The temperature in Chicago wasn't oppressive like it was in Las Vegas, which was kind of a nice change of pace.

Ricard got out on the other side, courtesy of one of the guards waiting for us. We were both motioned to step away from the car, another guard coming over with a wand to wave over us.

I didn't usually like going places with no weapons —it made me feel far too naked for my comfort—but as long as Ricard didn't let his mouth get him into trouble, we had a low chance of being stabbed.

Though low chance didn't mean no chance.

Good thing I was crafty and quick on my feet.

After getting cleared, another guard waved for us to follow him inside. I kept close to Ricard, acting like his own personal bodyguard as we stepped up the steps and into the foyer.

While I wanted my influence to seem nonexistent to the untrained eye, that also didn't mean I wanted to leave Ricard looking vulnerable. We were playing this game like chess, each of our moves highly calculated to ease these potential contracts into a false sense of security that could guarantee us a spot on their roster.

I didn't want us to come swinging out of the gate —that made for a bit of a desperate look. Not to mention like I'd told Ricard earlier, Liam's death was still fresh. If any of these families that we were going to be approaching in the upcoming weeks, especially the Rosettis's, had any healthy amount of awareness to them, they'd be taking everything with a grain of salt.

Which was smart on their part. It wasn't every day that a kingpin was taken out so unexpectedly. Not to mention with absolutely no telling as to what the fuck actually happened in the first place.

Only Ricard and I were privy to that knowledge. And like fuck we were letting any of that get out.

It only took one small whisper of gossip for it to spread like wildfire that Ricard was too much of a liability to work with. If everyone was scared of him taking them out like we had with Liam, then we'd be blacklisted before this game of ours even got started.

That couldn't happen. Not on my watch.

"Mr. Machiavelli." Both Ricard and I turned at the same time. "Don Rosetti is waiting for you. If you'll follow me."

Silently, I cheered the kid on while I slid my hands into my pockets. As apprehensive as I was to let him lead this ship on his own, I needed to be able to trust him with matters like this if we were going to have a successful partnership in the future.

I couldn't be stuck hand-holding him the entire time while trying to do my own shit. We not only had to get this off the ground, but I also needed to keep it under the radar from his father—a feat that was easier said than done.

Ricard Sr. wasn't a bumbling idiot, unfortunately,

and his wife even less so. Together, they made a formidable force that we'd need to be careful getting through. Especially if I wanted to keep myself as bullet-hole free as possible.

Ricard stepped away to join the consigliere who'd come and got him, leaving me to stand awkwardly with the three other guards who'd escorted us in. Giving them all a rather innocent smile, I spoke.

"Sooo, you guys got any cracker and cheese boards lying around here? 'Cause, I'm starving."

Hopefully at least a few rooms away so I can map out how this place is set up.

"I'll take him." A woman's voice chimed in, coming from across the foyer and up on the stairs leading to the second floor.

Turning to her, I put on my best winning smile. "Well, I didn't know I'd be escort by such a..."

My voice trailed off the moment I laid my eyes on her.

The woman. From the bar.

Who'd given me the worst case of blue balls I'd ever had in my life.

What the fuck?

She descended the stairs casually, her fingers running along the banister in a long swipe as she did so. I was so stunned to see her again that I barely registered my mouth hanging open until she was standing right in front of me, using her finger under my chin to snap it closed for me.

"Might want to keep that shut. Unless you like swallowing bugs."

Hoooolyyyy shit.

A familiar curl of heat settled into my gut.

"Well, well." I grinned. "If I knew I'd be seeing you again, I would've dressed nicer."

She gave me a slow once-over, her eyes lingering on my hands that were tucked in front of my waist. I also didn't miss the way her eyes flashed with something—heat, if I wanted to be delusional—before she stepped back from me.

"Miss Aylin," one of the guards addressed her. "Would you like us to escort him to the guest's waiting room?"

Aylin. Just a delicate name for such a tigress in disguise.

"No, I'll take him with me."

Trying to listen to the warning bells, while ignoring my very loud arousal, was a chore in itself.

My dick was loving the slow smile she gave me, the kind that promised to have those plush-looking lips wrapped around my already-becoming-a-problem hard-on. My brain, on the other hand, was screaming a series of questions at me that were hard to ignore.

One, why the *fuck* was she here?

Two, *how* the fuck was she here?

And three, this was obviously a distraction.

Okay, the last one wasn't so much of a question as it was a giant red flag waving itself in front of my face like I was a fucking bull trying to outrun the matadors.

This woman, *Aylin*, showing up here wasn't a coincidence. Not only that, but it seemed our meeting in New York had been predestined.

Had she planned to run into me and seduce me the entire time, or had I just been a happy accident? Either way: red flag.

"Come along." She spun on her heel, her long, curly hair flying over her shoulder.

God, I wanted to grab it so fucking badly.

I had a feeling if I tried, the guard behind me would be all too happy to twist my arms back behind me and snap my shoulders out of the sockets for even daring.

I wasn't going to lie, though; it was all the more tempting.

Following after her, I kept a good two feet between us as she led me down a hallway on the direct opposite side of where Ricard had gone off in. Making it as less conspicuous as possible as we walked, I internally mapped out the hallway, counting all of the doors we passed by until we got to one toward the end that she stopped in front of and opened.

Aylin nodded for me to step inside before coming in herself. Two of the guards that had followed us down the hallway were now stopped right outside of the room.

"Send for some refreshments," she told them both. "I'm sure they'll be a while."

They, as in Don Rosetti and Ricard. And whoever else the man had invited.

Not much was known about Gioni Rosetti, other than him being almost as young as Ricard and having the temperament of a rottweiler. His father, Giovanni Rosetti, on the other hand was a legend. Gioni had a lot to live up to if he ever hoped to one day outshine his late father.

Which was a perfect opportunity for Ricard and me to swoop in and promise the glory to him.

An "I scratch your back, you scratch mine" kind of relationship.

"Of course, ma'am," one of the guards said. "We'll be right back with those."

"Thank you," Aylin said, shutting the door once they were both out of the way.

I took that as my opportunity to take whatever chair looked the most comfortable and planted my ass right in it. The room wasn't that big, which meant it was probably only used for private entertainment. Another check on my box of Aylin most likely planning on seducing me.

Honestly, it was going to pain me to turn her down in order to keep my head on straight. I hadn't been able to get my mind off her since that stupid rundown bar in Brooklyn and her leaving me hanging—quite literally.

It wasn't fair for a beautiful woman like her to be walking around with that much power over a man. Maybe it was also my fault for getting myself too entangled with her to begin with. I should've trusted my gut in knowing she was a dangerous one with how out of place she looked in that bar.

Yet my dick had overpowered me.

And now I was stuck suffering with a halfsie while she seated herself in the chair across from me looking completely in control.

Must be nice.

Glancing around the room again, I spied a little camera up in the corner, partially hidden by a piece of the molding sticking out.

Iiiinteresting.

"So," I beat her to the punch. "Working with the Rosettis, huh? Didn't figure you for a mob kinda girl."

"Why's that?" She leaned back, crossing her leg over her knee. The move really showed off how tight those pants were.

"Well, not to sound like 'that guy,' but you don't really strike me as the type."

"No?" She smiled slowly, a devilish kind of amusement turning her eyes darker. "And what kind do I seem like?"

This has to be some test of my willpower, because my god.

"I wouldn't exactly say innocent. But..."

Honestly, I had no idea where any of this was going.

So far, she hadn't moved an inch from where she was sitting, which was a good eight feet away from me. Not a very good look if she was planning on seducing me. Not to mention, she'd asked her guards to bring back refreshments. Which meant she was planning on us being interrupted—checked on?—it was anyone's guess.

"I'm an assistant for the consigliere," she finally said. "I've only just begun working for the Rosettis. They've been very kind to me so far. How long have you been working for Mister Machiavelli?"

Now that was truly the million-dollar question, wasn't it?

"Not long," I finally settled on.

I had to say, I was surprised she was only an assistant. She obviously had bigger goals in mind, judging by the way she carried herself. I wondered what had wound her up in Brooklyn, then? If she was working for the consigliere and not the Don himself, that made me even more intrigued.

Typically the advisor wasn't one to give their own personal assistants assignments to go stalk people, but then again, it could've been a coincidence thing.

Who am I kidding, though? I don't believe in that shit.

Clearly the consigliere was looking into Ricard—and by proxy me—but why? We'd only just started making our moves.

Why were we already getting sussed out?

"You go by Max, right?" Aylin spoke up again.

"Guilty."

She smiled at me. "You can call me Aylin."

CHAPTER 2

Aylin

LOOKING OVER MAX GRAVES, I had to admit I kind of regretted telling my guards to come back to interrupt us.

It was a standard protocol that I'd put in place ages ago when entertaining new guests. One could never really tell how rowdy or bold they'd get in the company of someone like me who on the outside seemed non-threatening, when that couldn't be farther from the truth on the inside.

Having that small reminder in the back of the guests' heads that there would be two large men with guns coming back to "check" in on things was enough to keep most of them in line and me from having to serve out due punishment.

However, seeing the hard-on Max was trying his best to cover by covertly rearranging himself in his chair was making me want to text them both not to bother and that I had everything handled.

Usually, I wasn't one to give into the carnal pleasures of my enemy. Especially with my brother tending to the baby-Don of said enemy on the other side of the house.

But damn did Max do something for me.

It must be the way he didn't shy away from running his eyes over me, making it obvious how attracted he was to me. He did the same thing in the bar the night I'd stalked him down, his eyes locked onto me the moment I'd stepped away from the shadows.

It made my pussy tingle, knowing that he was that locked onto me and we hadn't even been introduced yet.

I'd been watching him for weeks at that point, keeping out of sight while I gathered whatever intel I could on the rogue Machiavelli heir and his bodyguard.

Us fucking hadn't exactly been on the agenda, but it had been a good way for me to see just how reckless the man in front of me could be if given the opportunity. He was a vulture—an opportunist. That spelled trouble for my family, especially if he and the Machiavelli heir were gung-ho about getting involved with us.

Which, apparently, they seemed very eager to do.

It made me wonder what kind of strife was going on within their ranks for one of their own to betray them by stepping out like that.

I couldn't trust a man that was impulsive—there

was no predictability in that. I wasn't interested in solving the unsolvable, especially when it came down to the safety and financial stability of my family.

But damn did I want Max Graves for my own personal pleasure. Use him like I had back in that hotel room. I hadn't had a body warming my bed in quite some time, and he seemed perfectly content with filling the job.

"Aylin." He tested my name out on his tongue. It rolled off it nicely. "That's pretty."

"Thank you." While playing coy usually got me somewhere, I was doing this for a different reason. "But you never really answered my question, though. From before."

He laughed. His long legs stretched out before him while he lounged further back in his chair. "What's with all the shop talk? Why don't we table that and get to know each other instead?"

His charm was rather good. I was sure if I was any other person, or woman for that matter, I would've fallen right into it and let him lead me down whatever conversation path he was trying to push. He was obviously wanting to interrogate me about something, just as I was trying to do to him.

Funny thing about that, though: we were in my territory. And I had been at this game a hell of a lot longer than he had.

"Bad habit I picked up from my boss."

He laughed again. "I can see that. Is he kind of a hard-ass?"

Frankie a hard-ass? That's funny.

"He can be," I lied. "I'm still new, so I'm trying to be on my best behavior."

Max flashed me a smile. "That must be quite challenging."

Fuck. I hate how much I want this man.

It was taking everything in me not to go over there and sit myself down right on his lap so that I could feel that huge cock dig into my ass. When I'd first had it, I'd been impressed by not only the length, but the girth he had on him. From looking at Max, you could never guess that he had practically a third leg hanging out in between his other two.

The shape of it had been practically imprinted inside of me from the way I kept remembering it each morning I woke up. I'd never craved a man's cock the way my pussy craved his.

I was already getting wet just thinking about it again.

Actually, maybe that would get me some answers. Max was clearly a chatterbox; if I got him to lower his guard enough, I could get him to talk.

I stood slowly, letting my body stretch out before him. Just as I predicted, he locked in on me, his stare only wavering just enough to take me all in.

I could tell he liked what he saw. Even if his eyes didn't do the talking for him—which they absolutely told me a novel's worth—that bulge in his pants certainly said enough.

I needed this. A good quick fuck wouldn't hurt.

And maybe I'd even be nice to him this time around and let him get off too.

Or maybe I'd be just as selfish as I was last time and force him to watch me cum on him, only for him to be denied the same pleasure. Call me sick and twisted, but I loved watching a man squirm, especially when his cock was still inside of me.

Just as I was about to step forward and cross the distance between us and make this fantasy I'd cooked up in my mind come to life, the door swung open.

One of my guards was standing in the doorway, looking rather frazzled. "Miss Aylin? The consigliere needs you."

Without meaning to, I whipped around and glared at him. *You've got to be fucking kidding me.*

This had better be fucking good.

CHAPTER 3

Ricard

SHAKING hands and sitting down at the table with Gioni Rosetti felt like a weird dream.

There were at least three of his guards inside of this conference room, along with three of mine. I'd wanted to show up with more, but Max had advised against it, his reasoning being that rocking the boat with such a show of force would make everyone uneasy.

While that was all fine and good, I didn't trust this guy as far as I could throw him. Not only was he around my age, but he also had a personality that I could only describe so far as unhinged.

"So I've been told you want to make a deal?"

Gioni sat with his legs tucked under him, his knees pressing against the side of the conference table in front of him. He had one of his elbows resting on a knee while his fist was carefully balancing his chin.

It reminded me of a kid that was bored at the adults' table, waiting—not so patiently—to be dismissed so that they could go play with their new toys they got for Christmas.

While I wasn't going to say out loud that Gioni seemed like a brat, he certainly had the superiority complex of one.

And that was saying something coming from me.

"We'd like to—"

I was cut off by Gioni speaking again. "We? Who's we?"

"Me and my business partner," I answered back coolly.

Max had coached me at least a dozen times by this point to keep from letting someone get a rise out of me. My temper was kind of impossible to check sometimes, but I was getting better. Slowly but surely. If I wanted this thing with Max to work, I needed to not fly off the handle like this guy was making me want to.

He frowned at me, his eyes glancing over to his consigliere, who was tucked into the corner of the room. "And who's that?"

"No one you need to be concerned about."

Gioni took his hand out from under his chin in order to slam it down onto the table. "I don't do business with shady people."

Isn't that the whole name of the game? That was what I wanted to counter with.

Thankfully, I was saved from my mouth flying by Gioni's consigliere stepping in. "Why don't we discuss that later? Right now, we want to focus on what exactly you bring to this potential partnership."

Okay, good. That was easy enough.

Ignoring Gioni's scowl thrown at his consigliere, I turned in my chair to grab the file outstretched to me. It was a list of benefits that Max and I had started rounding up weeks ago when I'd approached him about this project I'd had cooking in the back of my head for over two years.

While the list wasn't perfect, I knew I had some gold mines in there.

I handed it over to Frankie, Gioni's consigliere.

Next to him, Dante, his underboss, snagged it and handed it to Gioni.

Sitting back, I forced my posture to remain relaxed looking. I hated being here without Max, especially since this was the first time I was doing this shit on my own. I knew I had it in me; I'd been fucking bred for this. But Max was my safety crutch. He could read people better than I could read a damn book.

The tense atmosphere in here had me feeling apprehensive all of a sudden. Whether that was from Gioni's weird mood or something else in the water, I had no fucking clue. But as soon as we were out of here, I was forcing Max to go take me out to some backwoods part of this damn city to go shoot at something.

I needed to get this weird energy out of me.

Gioni flipped the papers loudly. "So... you want to get into business dealing products. Like what?"

I nodded. "I'm familiar with the fine jewelry trade,

but I'm interested in branching out. I have some good contact that can help with—"

Gioni cut me off again, making me fist my hands in my lap. "I already got a job for you."

I narrowed my eyes.

That was suspiciously fast. Not to mention a deal already? We hardly even talked. Wasn't there more to be hammered out before we started exchanging numbers and contacts?

The Machiavelli name was widely known, but guns were a different story. My father had already tried this once before, and it had crashed and burned before he even got it off the ground. Now he and my mother were in massive debt and fucking sunk to the damn trenches.

"What's the job?" I asked.

Gioni grinned. "We're receiving a shipment from a cartel over the border in Mexico. I need you to go pick it up. It's down in Arizona at the moment."

Cartel? What the fuck is this?

Cartels were serious business. Not only was that an area of trade that Max and I were trying to actively avoid for the time being, but we had no history with gunslinging in the first place.

And going into Arizona?

Well, I'd at least have home field advantage if I took on the job. Arizona and Nevada were neighbors, after all, and I'd traveled back and forth quite a bit over the last few weeks with Max looking for other families to connect with that we knew wouldn't slip back through the grapevine to my parents about.

I caught sight of the way Gioni's underboss shifted uncomfortably.

Would the Rosettis try and entrap me this early on? Moving weapons across state borders was difficult for sure, but as long as you had the right channels— which I didn't—you were golden.

I had contacts from my cousin to use as I saw fit per her blessing, but would she be able to help me with this?

"That's suicide," I finally said.

Gioni immediately scowled. "You think I'd set you up or something?"

"No," I said slowly, though I actually felt quite the opposite. I could feel the tension getting worse as his entire staff grew deathly quiet. "I mean that I have no contact with them. How are they going to trust me to take their supply?"

"I don't know," he snapped. "Figure it the fuck out. Isn't that what a consultant is supposed to do?"

Okay, apparently we'd gotten our wires crossed 'cause I wasn't a goddamn consultant.

The fuck?

"I want to have a business *contract* with you," I explained. "Not become your consultant."

He whipped around to glare at his consigliere. "Is this guy for fucking real?"

"Sir," Frankie cleared his throat, glancing over at

me briefly. "Why don't we take a lunch and come back to discuss things?"

"I have nothing I want to discuss. I was told I would be getting a consultant today, not a fucking... What do you want?"

I stared at him for a beat. Man, was I ever *this* annoying? If so, I needed to give Max a damn spa day. And maybe allow him a few right hooks to the face. "A *partnership*."

Gioni laughed. "I don't partner with anyone. So you think the Rosettis need their fucking hands held? Well, guess what? We've been doing this shit longer than you've been alive."

And there's the unhinged personality that I so famously heard about.

I should've just put up a fucking stink when they told me Max wasn't allowed in here. I couldn't believe I was dealing with this shit all on my own. It was taking every ounce of willpower not to fucking deck this guy right in the face and start a war.

"Look." I flattened my hands on top of the table, my fingers twitching slightly with how bad I wanted to curl them back up into firsts. "We can take a lunch—"

"I don't need a fuckin' lunch break," he spat at me.

If this guy cuts me off one more fucking time. I swear to god.

"All right." Dante stepped forward, placing a hard hand onto his boss' shoulder, hard enough to slap. "Since lunch is off the table, we'll reconvene at a later date."

"I'm only here today." I wasn't sticking around until man-baby over there got his shit together. I *also* had things to do. "So either we figure this out today or I'm headed back to Vegas."

Both the consigliere and underboss frowned.

"Fine then," Gioni snapped. "Walk. I don't give a fuck."

Immediately, I pushed up from my chair. There was no fucking way I was going to sit here and witness a temper tantrum from a man that was supposed to be running a conglomerate-sized syndicate.

Fuck that.

I neither had the time nor respect for that shit.

Frankie stepped away from his side of the table, holding out a hand. "Thank you for your time."

Yeah fucking right.

Once I got the chorus of goodbye handshakes out of the way, I had my guards lead me out of the room, nodding to one of them to go find Max. I wanted out of this fucking place *pronto*. I couldn't believe I let that bastard waste my fucking time.

Eventually, I met Max back in the foyer where we'd parted ways. He was standing there with a frown on his face, clearly wanting to know what happened to pull me out of my meeting so prematurely.

Next to him was a woman I didn't recognize.

As soon as she saw me, she stormed past me and down the hall to the conference room I'd just been in.

Wouldn't want to be in front of blocking her war path.

As we headed out into the fresh air, I breathed in slowly. "Fuck..."

"What happened?" Max muttered to me, nodding to the two guards standing on the front entrance's landing.

We stepped down together, both of our heads tucked in so we could speak softly as we waited for the car to be pulled around.

"He freaked out. Said he was expecting me to be his consultant."

Max's brow shot up. "He say why?"

I shrugged a shoulder. "Apparently he got the impression from either his consigliere or underboss. Don't know how that fucking wire got crossed."

"Hm..." Max leaned back from me, that familiar frown settling on his face.

As he got lost in whatever thoughts were running through his head, trying to piece together the fucking mindfuck of a puzzle that was now in front of us, I stared out at the lawn, waiting for our car.

While this had been my first time heading my own meeting, I felt a little disappointed it hadn't panned out like I'd wanted it to. I'd stressed the entire plane ride over here and then this morning at the hotel when we'd woken up.

I wasn't a fool to delude myself in seeking anyone's approval of me. Especially Max's. I'd long since realized that looking for that kind of thing was only making me weak as a future Don. All I needed was a reliable network and a close-knit circle, not to be begging for a pat on the back like I had when I was still a teenager.

As sad as it was to step out on my father, he was never going to see me as the man I wanted to be. If I stayed at the estate, I was always going to be forced to live in his shadow, regardless of whether or not he was still around for it.

The staff, my mother, his contacts, none of them were going to accept me. They would only be looking for the trace of my father that I still carried and rejecting me when they couldn't find it.

Nudging Max, I caught his attention again, just as the car was being parked in front of us. "I did find out something."

"What?"

"They were talking about getting us involved in some job. Picking up a supply of guns for them from the cartel."

Max's brows shot up again. "We don't deal with that shit."

"That's what I told them. He wasn't having it. That's when he had his little meltdown."

As Max stepped down onto the walkway leading to the driveway, I followed after him. "He sounds unstable."

"He fucking was. I couldn't get an entire sentence out before he was cutting me off and throwing a damn tantrum. His underboss practically had to hold his hand to calm him down. It looked like he was ready to swing."

Max grabbed the handle to the door of the car when he got close enough, swinging it open before he looked back at me. "I hate to say it, but maybe this was a bust."

"That sucks. They were the only contacts my parents hadn't dug their claws into yet."

"I know. But we'll keep looking. Their network is wide, but it's not infinite."

True, but that didn't give me any hope for the future.

Who knew starting your own syndicate was this fucking difficult?

Especially trying to go behind the back of your own maker?

Max nudged me with his shoulder, nodding for me to get into the car. "We'll talk about it on the way back. We'll come up with something."

I sure fucking hoped we did. If I had to deal with my father for another year, I was actually going to jump off the goddamn roof.

CHAPTER 4

Max

GETTING our shit together for the plane took less time than I thought it would.

Being that our meeting with the Rosettis had been cut so short, I saw no point in us sticking around longer than we had to. Ricard Sr. didn't have a clue as to where we were, so getting back home the quicker we could would work out better in the end anyway.

After we got home, Ricard and I would need to reconvene. While the Rosetti family hadn't been our be-all-end-all by any means, we'd had high hopes for them. Now that it was clear they were an unfit business partner, we were back to square one all over again.

We knew going into this that Gioni Rosetti was an unstable loose cannon as much as he was a hot head. It had been talked about almost like some kind of urban legend through the grapevine during our research into potential contacts. I just never figured he'd let it show so early on.

Then again, when you could wipe out entire legions of people with a snap of your fingers, that kind of power really did go to your head.

Piling back into the car, I settled back into the seat while Ricard lounged against the window, buried in whatever was on his phone.

I could tell he was upset, whether with himself or the situation, I wasn't exactly sure. But I still felt for him. It wasn't easy getting your hopes up and preparing for something like this, only for a 180 to hit and completely knock over your plans before they could even get off the ground.

I was sure he was mostly likely texting his cousin, filling her in on the details of what a psycho Gioni had been. The two had become rather close since this whole endeavor had started, and that was the kind of relationship I wanted him to cultivate.

I'd met her once before, and she'd seemed solid enough to rely on if things got sticky in the future.

Though I was iffy on trusting her completely—given that she was still under Ricard's father's thumb technically—but that didn't mean I didn't want Ricard to have his network. He'd need all the allies he could get once shit hit the fan and he eventually broke the news to his father that he'd be stepping away from the family to pursue his own interests.

When that day came, I wanted to be ready for it, though. There was nothing worse than a father like Senior losing his only heir and realizing his empire was slowly going to come crumbling down around him.

However, that's what he got for trying to clip his own son's wings before the kid could even properly leave the nest.

So. His karma, really.

As our driver, a big man named Jack, who had a scar similar to mine over his right eye down to his cheek, got into the front seat and put the car into gear.

I stared out my window at the moving city around us. While I didn't exactly miss the Las Vegas desert, I was certainly eager to go back to it. Chicago wasn't a bad place to wind up in, but knowing I was in the same city as Aylin gave me a strange feeling.

It was weird to me how... different she'd presented herself while at the Rosettis versus when we'd first met at that bar. Like she'd completely turned off her personality and was trying to be "good." For why, I had no fucking clue. She didn't strike me as the type to be scared of anyone, let alone her boss. And the excuse that she was trying to make a good first impression didn't sit right with me, either.

It all seemed too superficial for a woman like her.

Why bother going into a world like the mafia if you were too terrified to make any waves? With that mentality, she would've been better suited behind a desk in some cushy office building.

Here's the thing, though: she wasn't the type. I *knew* she wasn't because that look in her eyes—that hunger that I saw in Ricard's and in my own every single day when I looked in the mirror—was the same. It was obvious.

She couldn't hide that shit, no matter how hard she tried to.

She could play her little secretary duty to that consigliere all she wanted—I wasn't fucking buying it.

Not for a second.

"Shit," I heard Ricard mumble, looking out the back window. "Tail."

Fuck.

Twisting around in my seat, I looked through the window as well. Sure enough, a black SUV was tailing us, weaving in and out of traffic to keep up with us as Jack tried to lose them in the busy streets.

The other two guards we'd brought with us had left earlier to head to the airport to secure us seats for the next flight out of here, making us a little more vulnerable in this situation than I would've liked.

I was fine looking out for just me. Ricard, on the other hand, was a different story. He could hold his own, don't get me wrong, but in this kind of fight? I hadn't exactly trained him for flying bullets at the speed of seventy going down a freeway just yet.

Sue me. We had other shit that was more pressing.

Turning back around, I bent down to rip open the bag at my feet and get us a few guns, tossing two of them to Ricard.

"If this turns into a shootout," I said to Jack, "I want you to keep going."

"Got it," he said back to me, stepping on it as we got onto the freeway.

Pulling out my rifle, I checked the mags on it. Filled to the brim. Excellent.

"They're coming up fast," Ricard warned.

"Let 'em," I said, rolling down my own window.

If these fuckers wanted a gunfight, then they were going to get one.

They ended up pulling right up next to Ricard's side—two guys who looked vaguely familiar from the staff that I could recognize inside of the Rosettis' estate. Ricard pointed his gun out the window, firing off two rounds to the driver's side window, shattering it.

"Nice," I complimented. "Go for their tires next."

We'd get them off the road one way or the other.

A couple of shots were fired back at us, causing Ricard and me to duck down to keep from getting sprayed with them. One of the bullets managed to shoot through the cabin and hit the side of the door closest to my arm.

Fuckers.

"Hey," I called to Jack. "Pull us off the highway. I want to see if we can catch them and see who sent them."

"Isn't it obvious the Rosettis did?" Ricard said, pointing his gun out the window again and getting another shot out.

"Duck," I told him, lifting up from my crouched position in order to aim my rifle out through the window.

He practically dove for the floor as I fired off

rapidly, leaving a nice long trail of bullet holes along the front lip of the SUV's hood. The sound of tires squeaking and the car jerking back out of view had me grinning.

"Yeah, but we need confirmation," I told him. "We can't go accusing them of shit if we have no proof. They can just as easily pin it on someone else."

He grunted at me but didn't argue further.

I gotta say, I was proud of him. Keeping his cool during that meeting, keeping his cool now, even when I was straight-up disagreeing with him. He'd turned over a whole new leaf in the span of a few months.

I was proud of him, to be honest.

Like my kid brother was finally growing up and shaping up into a man.

"They're coming up on the left, Graves," Jack spoke up, careening over to the right lane to get off on the next exit.

Twisting back around to look out the rearview, I spotted the SUV coming up on him hot while swerving in and out of traffic.

"Take us to a back alley. Closest one you see. We need to get these shitheads off the road before the police catch us all," I told him.

"Roger that."

The car jerked, sending both Ricard and I plastered against my side of the cab. He grunted at my gun digging into his chest, his hand coming out to slap down onto the side of my door to push himself upright.

"Fuck. If I have an imprint of your fucking toy by the end of this, I'm going to be pissed."

I smirked at him. "What's wrong with having my M4's logo tattooed on you?"

"Fuck that and fuck you," he spat back, double-checking his own clip.

The car stopped hard at the light down at the end of the exit, almost slamming into the line of cars in front of us. I braced myself with my leg out to keep from pitching forward into the seat in front of me. While I was sure I could pull off the "no teeth" look, I really wasn't interested in testing it out.

Cranking the wheel around, Jack pulled the car off onto a worn patch of dirt next to the line, giving us enough room to move up and take a right without having to wait.

I had no doubts that our tail was going to be following right after us, but we needed to be quicker. As long as we were able to trap them, we could take them out before they could get us.

Jack drove for half a mile down the main strip of whatever city we were in until he took a hard right. I grabbed onto Ricard's shoulder before he could smack into me—and the rifle pressed to my chest—and held him upright.

See, that was the downfall of being a thin kid: you were too easily thrown around like a rag doll.

I needed to see about getting him bulked up. It'd definitely help with the intimidation factor later on down the line.

Before I knew it, Jack had us pulled off of the road and into a covered alley, wedged between two tall buildings that practically blocked out the sun.

Nice.

Popping open my door just enough to face my gun out of it, I waited, hearing Ricard do the same on his side. It wasn't more than two minutes later before a familiar SUV was pulling its way down the alley, lights off.

Both Ricard and I fired at the car.

Bullets went flying, littering the front windshield as well as blowing at the tires. The SUV came to a hard stop as the front tire exploded first. Whoever was driving tried to K-turn out of the alleyway but only got themselves wedged in between the two buildings like a ham sandwich.

The second both doors popped open, Ricard fired off four rounds, getting the passenger twice in the shoulder and leg and the driver right in the middle of his back.

I grinned as I watched them both fall to the ground. "Nice one, kid."

He scoffed at me. "Yeah, yeah."

Awww, my little sharpshooter.

"Jack, call for backup. We're going to need a cleaner here before the police arrive."

"Got it," he said.

Getting out of the car, I set my rifle down onto the back seat, catching one of the handguns Ricard tossed to me over the trunk before walking toward the fucked-up car and the two bodies on the ground.

Blood was already pooling under the passenger's body, his groans of pain both loud and obnoxious.

I kicked him right in the teeth, the force of my boot meeting his head snapping his neck back and conking him right out.

"Should we shoot him?" Ricard raised his gun.

I shook my head. "Let's see what the driver has to say first. I want answers."

CHAPTER 5
Max

UNFORTUNATELY, we didn't get much.

"Fuck you!" the man spat at us, blood already gurgling up his throat from where the bullet had been lodged into his back and probably piercing one of his lungs. "I ain't tellin' you shit!"

I stepped on his back, right over his wound. He let out a groan of agony. "How about now?"

"Fuuuuck!" he choked out.

"You working for the Rosettis?" I asked.

He gurgled on his next response, blood dripping out of his mouth and onto the pavement below him.

Ew...

Ricard sighed. "I doubt they'll tell us anything."

He was probably right, which sucked.

While we probably wouldn't get anywhere accusing the Rosetti family of sending a tail after us trying to take us out, that didn't mean the information couldn't be used for a later date.

For the reason as to why any of this was happening, I couldn't really imagine. Because Don Rosetti was embarrassed by his own behavior? Doubt that. Maybe one of his inner circle had been instead? Possible. Cleaning up the mess of their Don looking like a fucking lunatic? Most likely.

But who really knew?

In any case, what mattered was that clearly the Rosettis found us as a liability that they needed to get rid of. Going so far as to send someone after us to do the job was something I'd definitely need to remember if we were going to be potentially poaching any of their contracts once we got ourselves settled somewhere else.

There were only so many fish in the big pond of the underground. At some point, we were going to be crossing wires and whoever the best contact for hire came out on top, that's who'd be getting the pick of the crops.

"Gioni seemed unstable enough to do something like this," Ricard said, leaning over the hood of the SUV to check on the passenger who was still lying unconscious. "I have a feeling he probably sent these guys to take us out."

I raised a brow. "You really think so? He knows about your family, though."

"Look, it's not about that. If he was that offended about me telling him I was interested in a contract and not being his consultant, imagine what other shit he was thinking after I told him we were leaving since we didn't get what we came here for. He's the kind of hothead to get it all up in his head that us walking out was some kind of personal dig."

That... actually was a good point. While Ricard had a history of being a hothead himself, Gioni was taking it to a whole new level if this was indeed his stunt.

That man... there was something wrong with him.

"Don't suppose you have any preference on how we get rid of these bodies?" I smirked at him. Okay, maybe I was testing him to see if he knew the protocol, so sue me.

I needed to keep my boy sharp.

He rolled his eyes at me before shaking his head ruefully. "Clean-up crew should do that job."

"I got Jack on it. But let's get these assholes out of sight before someone comes strolling along and sees us with them."

"Sure thing."

After Ricard took both kill shots, we piled the bodies into the back of the SUV and waited until a local cleaner crew came to grab it and take it away.

While I was sad to part ways with a cool fifty grand for the cleanup, I had to commend them on their quick and easy removal. They even had a guy come around with a street sweeper to get up all the blood that the driver had coughed up.

Before we all knew it, the place looked better than how it started.

Jack eventually had us get back into the car and drove us to the airport, which was surprisingly the smoothest portion of this entire trip. The only shit part was having to wait in the terminal for our damn plane to start boarding.

That was the only thing about having to do the whole commercial thing—fucking waiting around for everyone else.

Taking the private jet would've been too risky, though. Even though it was ten times more convenient, I wasn't willing to let Senior catch wind of my and his son's dealings. Not so soon into it. We didn't have proper footing to keep us up if something were to try and topple us over.

Not at this stage anyway.

Not to mention I'd sooner find a Glock square between my eyes. That day would come eventually, but I hoped that by the time the death bell tolled, I'd have Ricard's network to back me to keep that from actually coming to fruition.

But even that was a long time from now. So patience was unfortunately a virtue at this stage.

"You know what?" I said after Ricard's third time going through his emails. "I think when we get home, we should figure out how to cool things with Gioni."

He slowly looked up from his phone. "What...? You can't be serious. He just tried to take us out."

"Allegedly," I reminded him. "And think about it. The guy's unstable. You said so yourself."

"Yeah... and?"

"*And*," I turned in my seat to face him, the hard arm from my chair digging into my back, "even if we can hide all of this from your father, the guy's clearly pissed off enough at whatever offended him. We need to smooth things over with him before word gets back to your parents about this."

His eyes widened briefly, the information sinking in. "You don't think he'd go that far to declare war... do you?"

I shrugged. "From what you told me, I doubt his underboss would let that happen. But that doesn't mean there won't be chattering. If your parents found out you even went to meet with another family, they're going to want to know why. Hate to break it to you, kid, but you're horrible at lying to them."

He made a face. "I've gotten better."

I smirked. "Sure. But that doesn't mean they can't read you like a damn book. Look, I know it's not ideal, but we're going to have to suck it up for the sake of saving our own skin. I don't want that guy after us anymore than you do. Right?"

He sighed. "I guess..."

"Plus, who knows when we'll run into him in the future. All the more reason to smooth things over in a week or two once he's cooled off. Maybe he'll even reconsider our offer once it's brought up again."

"Doubt that, but I can try. I'm sure his people will

have talked to him by then, though. They didn't seem to want to say anything to him while I was there, but I doubt they would tolerate that behavior."

Something in me told me that that wasn't exactly accurate, but maybe that was just me being pessimistic and speculating on the subject because I really couldn't see Aylin standing there while a man that appeared almost ten years younger than her pitched a fit like a fucking toddler.

What I *could* see her doing was going over there and knocking some sense into her Don.

Quite literally.

Though who knew? Maybe she was actually only confident in the bedroom.

That would be so disappointing if that happened to be the case, not gunna lie.

But all of this was making me second-guess everything.

Fuck, I hated when that happened.

"When we get home, we can go over what I should say to him." Ricard brought his phone back up to his face.

"Sounds good to me. Hey, while you're at it, see what your cousin can dig up on the Rosettis."

His fingers started flying over the screen. "You got it."

The only thing worrying me now was wondering whether this was going to be the end of our Gioni and Rosetti family saga or if this entire mess was only just the beginning.

CHAPTER 6

Aylin

A FEW DAYS after Max and his Machiavelli brat had left the estate, I'd gotten word that their tail had come up MIA.

It wasn't unheard of for my teams to go under-cover in order to pull out a successful hit—even though this time around, it hadn't been that kind of mission, but whatever needed to be done needed to be done, so I never held it against them in the end. So after the first two days of hearing nothing, I hadn't assumed the worst.

Now that it was going on a solid four days and no whisper of communication between my tail and our control center, I was beginning to suspect something might have happened.

Max, of course, being my number-one suspect.

I hated the way my pussy clenched at the thought of him. What a fucking nuisance that was all becoming.

It wasn't until a day after *that* that I finally got confirmation of said suspicion and the discovery of not only the SUV my men had left in but their DNA scrubbed off of every inch of the inside of it.

I immediately knew without a doubt that the professionals had been called in to clean the scene.

Fuck, I really don't have time to be dealing with this right now.

With the deal between my brother and Ricard Machiavelli going completely sideways, I had enough on my plate that I had to focus on that didn't involve tracking down an damn ex-ops member who seemed to be dipping his damn fingers into anything he could get his hands on.

What his interest in any of this was was really beyond me. It wasn't typical of an ex-military member to get involved with the underground's dealings. Their sensibilities were much too sensitive for this kind of stuff. Growing up in it was one thing, but coming into it as fresh meat typically never went over well.

I regretted letting him get away from me. I'd bitten off more than I could chew by taking myself out of the room and trusting Gioni to handle Machiavelli Jr.—something that I was never going to do ever again—while I handled his watch dog.

I normally always took control of things by myself, but I'd been too intrigued by Max showing up with a mafia prince at his side that my need to get to the bottom of it had won out over my need for control over my brother. What I didn't account for was the rest of my fucking team to be absolutely useless as well.

What the fuck were any of them doing, anyway? What the fuck did I pay them for?

My underboss, my damn consigliere, and even my fucking caporegimes had disappointed me in the end.

I swore. No one could do this fucking job without me hand-holding them.

There was a knock at my office door, bringing me out of my thoughts.

"Miss Aylin?"

I sighed and lifted my head up from the mountains of paperwork in front of me, glaring at the closed door. It sounded like Dante.

"What?"

"There's been an update on that shipment coming from Mexico."

Jesus, what now?

"Come in," I said, pushing back from my desk in order to stand.

The door swung open, revealing the Rosetti underboss standing in the doorway. He was a handsome man with a clean-shaven face and his hair gelled back to the side to show off his perfectly straight sidepart. His suit was perfectly pressed, and not a single crease could be seen on it.

When I'd first accepted Dante as the role for our underboss, I'd taken that need for perfectionism into account. As the one keeping things behind the scenes together while I went out and worked my magic, he was supposed to be the one making sure that ship kept running smoothly.

The keyword there was *supposed to be.*

What happened with my brother was fucking abysmal. We all knew Gioni was a loose cannon and could go off with that short temper of his, but with the right kind of hand guiding him into not being so hot headed, he worked well.

Which was exactly what Dante's fucking job was supposed to be.

I was too busy to manage my brother's unstable emotions, especially when I was trying to figure out why the fuck an ex-ops military killing machine was inside of my damn house.

"What's the problem?"

Dante hesitated in the doorway before heading into my office and swinging the door shut behind him.

I didn't like the way he was looking like he wanted to avoid talking to me about whatever was going on. I had a habit of not taking bad news well, mainly because my plans of operations were nearly flawless. The only instance of things not panning out were people either refusing to do what they had been assigned to *or* outside interference.

Other people were always my biggest fucking prob-lem, hence why if I could, I'd do everything myself.

"There was a problem with that shipment of weapons coming into Arizona from Mexico. Seems that someone's intercepted it."

"*What?*" I snapped.

Impossible.

Who the fuck would do that unless they wanted to lose their fucking head?

Actually: who would be *stupid* enough to do that and *not* think they'd lose their fucking head?

"We're not sure of the details. Alex is looking into the CCTV footage to track down where it disappeared to."

Leaning forward, I placed my hands flat against my desk. Breathing in deeply, I tried to reel back the anger waging inside of me. "What do you mean 'disappeared'?"

He hesitated again.

"Speak. Dante." I gritted through my teeth.

The man cleared his throat. "When our crew went out there to collect the shipment this morning, they found the entire loading dock full of workers dead. Seemed to have been some kind of takeover that they weren't expecting."

"Where the hell was security?"

He frowned. "Shot, ma'am."

I slammed my fist down onto the desk, rattling some of the things on top of it. How the hell did an entire crew get wiped out so easily without so much as a peep out of anyone? Including law enforcement. While I didn't typically like to deal with the cops or the feds, that didn't mean I didn't have eyes and ears within their ranks.

Especially when it came to situations where I needed to keep a close eye on production of imports and exports. I couldn't be in two places at once, and with Arizona and Nevada being over three thousand miles away, it made it nearly impossible to have a consistent amount of communication between myself and the crew down there on a regular basis.

If something or someone had been tipped off about this, I should've heard about it.

"All of them?" I asked, even if I was already guessing the answer.

"Yes, ma'am."

Fuck me sideways.

None of this could be a coincidence.

Max Graves showing up in my goddamn city with a Machiavelli under his wing, their tail going mysteriously missing, and now my entire crew being taken out soon after. Not to mention Nevada was where the Machiavellis lived, if I recalled.

It couldn't be chance. There had to be some inner workings here that I was missing.

But how the hell did they get down there so quickly in order to take my entire crew out *and* steal the damn shipment without anyone else being the wiser?

Was their visit here a distraction while a plan had been in the works? How the fuck did they find out about that shipment of weapons in the first place?

I kept my shit locked down tighter than the Pentagon.

"Miss Aylin." Dante cleared his throat, pulling me from my thoughts. "We're already setting up travel to get down there and assess the situation. I have a team of associates down there right now cataloging everything. I wanted to let you know that we were heading out soon if you wanted to join us."

I let out a slow breath.

I should be staying here in order to hold down the fort after that disaster with my brother, but this was a more pressing matter. Even if my suspicions were correct and the Machiavellis had something to do with this, I couldn't exactly send my men to their doorstep demanding answers.

I needed proof first, and that was going to come in the form of me getting myself into that damn compound. A meeting with the head of the Machiavelli family could get me in the door at least. After that, I'd need to figure out how to weasel the information that I wanted out of him.

Whether any of them, if they were guilty, would admit to the crime or not was of little value to me. So long as I could prove they took down my operation without a shadow of a doubt, then I had free rein to do whatever I felt was necessary in order to rectify the situation, an eye-for-an-eye type deal that would not only ensure my satisfaction but would keep me from taking more drastic measures such as taking out their entire family by the way of my handgun like my fingers were itching to do right at the moment.

Perhaps at the end of all of this, I'd have Max Graves under my thumb too. I certainly wouldn't mind ripping him away from that family and putting

SIMONE FOX

him inside of a cage where he belonged. No one needed that kind of power walking around without some kind of leash.

Pushing away from my desk, I walked around it and toward the door. Paperwork would need to wait. Until I had this mess resolved, at least.

"I'll meet you all downstairs in ten."

Dante followed after me, close behind while swinging my door shut once more when we stepped out into the hallway.

"Of course, ma'am. I'll have a car pulled up for you."

I nodded to him and then headed down the hall.

Time to go find Gioni and tell him to behave or else he's going to wish he'd kept his damn mouth shut at that meeting.

CHAPTER 7

Max

THE MINUTE our plane's wheels hit the tarmac, we were summoned back to the compound.

I didn't know why it didn't surprise me that there was a car waiting for us as soon as we were through security and back out into the desert heat of Las Vegas, but for some reason I had had a gut feeling as soon as our plane had hit thirty thousand feet up in the air that this would happen.

Whether or not Senior suspected Ricard and I to have met with another family was beside the point by now. All we needed to do was focus on not letting ourselves be caught red-handed that we were starting something behind his back, regardless of whether or not the Rosettis would even be interested in further contact.

Which... was easier said than done.

I was sure that whatever reason Ricard Sr. had sent a car to come pick us up with was going to either be about us leaving the state in general or leaving without a word of what we were doing that led us to leave in the first place.

He was controlling like that, especially when it came to his heir.

A funny thing about that, though, was that any other time Ricard was around on the estate's property, his father couldn't give two shits about what the kid was doing. It was almost like as long as his son stayed within the bounds of his property line, he was content with keeping him on a shelf.

And what a fucking waste that was.

I could tell by the time both of us climbed into the car and got ourselves buckled in that Ricard was apprehensive. He and I both knew that whatever was waiting for us back at the family estate was going to be some kind of shitstorm. Things often went unnoticed around there—which was why this little pick up was such a big deal.

If we'd done something to alert either of Ricard's parents that we'd left, then I wanted to know what the fuck it was so when next time came around, I'd have that shit patched.

"I think we should come up with something to tell him," Ricard muttered to me as his driver climbed into the front seat, starting the engine. "My dad's going to want to know where the fuck we were."

That was the tricky part about all of this: we had to walk the line of truth to make it believable. Not only were we toeing the line of betrayal, but if Senior suspected me of covertly taking his son away from him, I was a fucking goner.

No amount of me showing him evidence of my innocence would be enough to convince him otherwise. That man was steadfast in his beliefs and carried it around with him like a badge of integrity.

Not to mention Ricard's mother, Gianna, was stubborn as all hell. If *she* got it in her head, I'd be lucky to get two feet without a hole being blown straight through my damn chest.

Bleeding out on the floor of the Machiavellis' was definitely not on my bucket list, I'd say that much.

"He's going to want you to tell him," I told Ricard, leaning back into my seat to look at ease while his driver glanced at me in the rearview.

Ricard simply grunted at me.

This much was obvious to both of us.

If we were indeed on our way to an interrogation, Ricard was going to need to answer for both of us. In the eyes of his father, mother, and the rest of their inner circle, I was simply the help. Nothing more. I was only there as a means of being a meat shield if anything was to get in the way or threaten my charge.

My presence was otherwise supposed to go completely unnoticed.

While this had never been my preferred type of job, it had been a nice change of pace from the military when I first signed my contract. It had been a bitch and a half with convincing Caleb to come join me when we'd first started all of this. But now he was on the other side of the damn planet, so here I was feeling the aftereffects of being dogshit bored at trying to pretend to be part of the damn wallpaper most days.

Hence the need for my little pet project.

I hated to think it, but maybe Caleb had been right all along in side-eyeing me when I'd suggested we work as bodyguards for a local mafia ring.

"I'll tell him we took a trip," Ricard finally said, crossing his arms over his chest. "If I keep it simple, he won't have room to ask more questions."

I nodded to him.

It was a smart move—give his father nothing to work with and he would have less than what was ideal to pick apart. Senior had never struck me as the overly curious type, so hopefully whatever way Ricard was planning on spinning our story would get him off our backs long enough to come up with some other distraction to get his attention focused elsewhere.

The only other problem that stood in our way was Gianna herself.

She, I knew, would have questions and wasn't going to let Ricard off the hook that easily.

"Keep your mother in mind," I told him under my breath.

The last thing we needed was for her to unravel our plan and get Senior to bring down the hammer.

"Got it," he muttered back and then took a play from my book and relaxed back into his seat.

"Don Machiavelli has requested for both up to his office," Ricard's driver said the second we were parked outside the front doors of the estate.

As we both slid out of our seats and back out into the desert heat, I sighed to myself before stretching my arms over my head. It wasn't often that I felt like I was walking into the type of situation that was likely going to end in me dead, but then again, I had often gotten myself out of trouble more times than I could count.

These kinds of deeds were never left unpunished, especially while dragging someone else into the fray with me. But hey, that was where all the fun of it lay right?

Heading inside, we were both greeted with two men that I recognized as Senior's cousins. They were two older men that had salt-and-pepper hair and full beards that made them look almost identical to each other aside from one of them wearing glasses.

Their names, though? I couldn't give two fucks.

Without a word to either of us, both men turned and headed up the stairs leading to the second floor. I brushed my shoulder with Ricard's, motioning silently for him to head up first as I trailed behind.

While this felt like I was heading to my own execution, I couldn't help but feel a sense of thrill racing through me. Danger was the driving force behind many of my actions lately. I was an adrenaline junkie at heart, and this was all one big dose of dope for my system.

Did I think myself capable of making it out of this

alive if things went south side? Fuck yes. But it was going to probably leave me looking a little bit like swiss cheese.

My only regret would be forcing myself to leave Ricard behind. I'd grown attached to the kid, whether I liked it or not. I had a soft spot for him, and having to leave him behind to clean up our mess was going to be hard if it came down to it.

At the end of the day, I wasn't willing to die for him like his parents thought I was.

Though that certainly didn't mean I wouldn't be coming back for him. Eventually.

What could I say: when I become attached to things I liked, I kept them around.

As we came up the stairs, I could already tell Senior's office door was open by the light spilling onto the carpet outside of it. A positive sign, really, considering the man was usually a shut-in most days. If his office door was already open, that meant he was in a good enough mood for people walking by to pop their head in and chat.

Maybe we weren't in trouble after all.

Ahead of me, Ricard blew out a slow breath. I could see from here how tense his shoulders were, and while I didn't blame him for the reaction to having to face his father, I needed him to shape the fuck up. If he went in there acting like a guilty kid, then that's exactly how they were going to treat him, and then we'd be actually fucked.

Just as I was about to nudge him again, he

surprised me by rolling his shoulders back and lifting his head up from where he'd been glaring down at the carpet. He walked through the doorway with his head held high and a firm set to his jaw.

I grinned to myself before forcing myself to smoother it.

That's my boy.

"Junior!" his father called out to him the moment his feet hit the carpet inside of the office. "Ari, why did you bring him up here? I said I wanted him down in the basement."

Basement? I thought. *That's not good.*

The only things down in the basement were the interrogation room and the vault.

One of Senior's cousins cleared his throat—the one with the glasses. "My mistake, Don—"

"Was I not clear?" Senior growled, waving his hands at both his son and me. "Basement."

Shit.

I glanced over at Ricard, taking in his immovable expression as he stared at his father.

"Why do we have to go down here?" he asked. "Your office is perfectly fine."

As Ricard spoke, I glanced around Senior's office. No Gianna in sight. At least we had that much going for us.

"I have something I need to show you." Senior's tone was much more upbeat than I would've figured him to be, forcing me to turn my attention back onto him just in time to catch his grin. "Come on."

Heading out to the office, we were escorted with Senior at the head of our party and the two cousins bringing up the rear, with both Ricard and I smashed together in the middle. As I stared down his father's back, I couldn't help but feel a weird sense of foreboding.

Ever since the diamond fiasco a few months ago, Senior had been acting... strange. At the time, I'd chalked it up to the loss in serious funds as being the driving force behind his rather odd decision making. It was obvious that the entire situation had hit the family hard and had bestowed a seed of distrust within their network of buyers and dealers that had pushed them out to the outskirts of the other syndicates.

Not to mention that at the time, Liam had also been breathing down their necks about recouping his own losses.

So it was fair to say that *something* was going on, but I couldn't quite put my finger on it.

I got my answer the second we all descended into the basement and headed in the opposite direction of the interrogation room that I'd only had the pleasure of seeing inside of once before when I'd mouthed off to one of Senior's associates who'd turned out to be a fucking local politician in his pocket.

I had to say, for a prissy-bitch who seemed like all he did was sit behind a desk all day with his thumb up his ass, the guy had a mean right hook.

I could appreciate that in a man, honestly.

"I've been waiting for you to get back," Senior was

saying as he punched the code in for the vault, the doors of which swung inward. "I'm going to need your help with this."

Suspicious on top of suspicious. So he'd noticed we were gone but for some reason wasn't caring. Clearly whatever had been taking up his attention was enough to bypass any possessive tendencies the man had over his heir.

"Oh?" was all Ricard answered his father back with.

Subtle, yet conveyed exactly the type of "*the fuck?*" emotion I was also thinking.

As we stepped into the vault, lights overhead clicked on, illuminating the space around us. It was a large room with cement walls—completely impenetrable with any kind of sensory machinery that would be able to detect what was inside of it. *This* was a room inside of the estate I'd actually never been in.

Looking around, I could see that the room we were standing in wasn't the only thing behind that two-ton steel door. There was also a thin hallway, about two men shoulder-to-shoulder in width, that contained rows and rows of lock boxes with gold-lettered attachments interfaced on the outside of them.

If I had to guess, I'd give it a good hundred-dollar wager that this was where they were keeping their tangible funds. Not many families did that sort of thing anymore—most of them had begun to pivot to the more modern ways of crypto and off-shore cash accounts. But the Machiavellis were an old-school sort of group that relied heavily on the fact that their words and promises were backed by actual product.

Hence the need for a vault like this.

Senior moved across the room, heading over to the only other steel door that was planted into the wall opposite of us. He punched in another code before swinging it inward.

Over his shoulder, Ricard gave me a look that said a good "*what the fuck?*"

I shrugged at him. Like I had any fucking clue what his father had gotten himself into.

I hung back a few paces as Ricard followed after his father, ducking inside of the other, smaller room before disappearing inside. Behind me, I glanced back at the cousins, both of which were staring me down.

Kinda funny that they were giving me such hairy eyeballs when I could end them right here and now with no sound, no weapons, and with barely breaking a sweat.

Hm, the thought is really tempting.

Too bad I wanted to keep this job for a little while longer.

Since neither of them was telling me to leave the Machiavellis alone, I followed in after them. Curiosity was one day going to be the death of me, I was sure, but thankfully today wasn't going to be that day.

I had a long ways to go before that happened, hopefully.

The room was more of a storage unit that was an off-shoot from the main part of the vault and about a quarter of the size as well. In the center of the room was a single steel table, bolted down to the cement floors by the looks of it. Nothing was on it, making the surface of it reflect annoyingly bright from the lights above.

Looking away from it, I turned my attention to the walls surrounding us, not at all expecting what I was currently seeing.

Rows and rows of guns, all lined up in a uniform manner with their stocks faced outward and their barrels hooked between tight-framed rests.

"Holy fuck," I heard Ricard breathe out.

I blinked in surprise at the entire scene. There had to be at least a hundred or so. By the looks of it, it was probably close to two hundred.

Senior turned to us both, grinning widely. "Look what I found."

Found? I wanted to say. *More like stolen. No one finds this kind of cache laying around.*

Just what the fuck had Senior gotten himself into?

CHAPTER 8

Aylin

GETTING DOWN to Arizona was a quick and simple process—much more than what I encountered when I finally got to the warehouse that had been subsequently raided a few days prior.

While I wasn't exactly surprised to see that the entire place was a goddamn mess, I *was* interested in how messy the job seemed to have been. Almost as if this entire plan had come about as either a last ditch effort or the result of an impulsive decision.

Not only were guns that weren't ours left behind from the scuffle with their serial numbers scratched, there were also a few bodies that whoever had come and raided the warehouse had never bothered to come back to clean up before my associates got to do an entire sweep of the place to catalog everything.

It came as no surprise that none of the men left behind had any forms of ID on them—common in our line of work.

Most mafia didn't carry that sort of thing, especially if there was a chance that law enforcement would become involved at some point or another. Even if you didn't get taken out in the crossfire of a gunfight, no one wanted to give up their identity to the police in the off chance that something happened and arrests were made. Getting the family you worked for in hot water was a giant no-no, after all.

Any associate worth their salt knew that, which by the looks of it, all of them did.

Which made this all the more strange. My hunch that the Machiavellis being behind this was starting to teeter toward the "not" end of the spectrum. There were too many mistakes, too many pieces of evidence left behind that a seasoned family like that would've never let slip out from under them.

All of this was much too sloppy for a family that was known for being uptight within the syndicate circles.

While I had no knowledge of what they had dealings in before Max and the younger Ricard had showed up on my doorstep, I had a hard time believing that it was anything that had to do with firearms. Handling the cartels and arms dealers were no joke and took a certain kind of charisma that was only cultivated through years of doing this kind of shit.

My family had been on this side of things for longer than I'd been alive and had connections that spanned not only decades but across continents.

Drugs and guns were among the top investments

when it came to making serious money, but it also left you much more vulnerable to this kind of shitshow.

Not only was I out a serious amount of profit, but I was going to have to explain to the cartel I'd bought these guns from why half their fucking crew was dead among my own. While I wasn't afraid of answering to them in the slightest, their methods were often unpredictable, and right now I had no time to deal with a tantrum-fueled shitstorm.

"Miss Aylin." One of my associates came around from the other side of the docks, a tablet in his hands. "We got word from one of the cops who came across the scene initially. He's got CCTV footage of the guns being taken and put into a couple of SUVs before they took off with everything."

I grabbed the tablet out of his hands, flicking my finger over the glossy surface to scroll through still images that had been taken from the feeds that had been sent over. The footage was grainy and lacked anything definitive that could point us in a single direction other than the vans being a distinct gray color.

"License plates? Car make? What do we have so far?" I asked.

He hesitated before saying, "Well, we have a partial license plate number—"

I tuned him out the second the words fell out of his mouth.

Jesus, if this couldn't get any worse.

My finger found the button on the side of the tablet, shutting off the screen. I reached up to run my fingers over my brow bone, feeling the pressure headache already starting to bloom.

"What *do* we have?" I bit out.

"Unfortunately not much. There was a positive ID on one of the men who'd participated in stealing our supply. He's being held in county jail over in Nevada at the moment on another existing charge. Cops picked him up this morning."

Fuck, at least it was something. Though I doubted the guy would talk.

Couldn't hurt to go pay him a visit, though.

I slapped the tablet against my associate's chest, feeling slightly satisfied when he let out a pained grunt.

"Get me a car. I want go over there now."

Nevada county jails were hardly a sight to behold.

Not only was Boulder City a fucking shithole of a city, but it ran like a backward town that had fuckall to do and time to waste. Which absolutely drove me insane. I hated time wasted and inefficiency when it came to getting things done.

Especially if I needed it done quickly.

It took a little over an hour—and a hefty fat stack of cash—to get the cops to agree to let me in to see the associate that had been caught and detailed. Places like this always ran on some ridiculous moral code that not only pissed me off but made me want to burn the entire precinct down.

Everyone had a price, and it wasn't hard to find it most days. But apparently the cops that worked in this god-forsaken city liked to pretend to have morals that made bribing them all that more annoying.

This situation was turning out to be more of a headache than I'd hoped it would be. I'd planned on getting down to the bottom of this, catching who'd done it, and dragging them back to the comfort of my estate to be tortured in my basement for the rest of their natural life.

Yet here I was, stuck in some dinky little interrogation room with a man that was around my height and build and was staring at me like I was the hottest thing that had hovered in his vicinity since the last stone age.

"Wow." He smirked at me. "Didn't know they'd be sending in a smokin' hot babe to—"

I slapped him right across the mouth, cutting off whatever annoying compliment he was about to hurl at me.

He choked out a surprised grunt of pain, clearly shocked by my reaction to him.

Honestly, what the fuck did he expect? I knew I had not only a resting bitch face, but my mood was sour enough that it would be obvious. I never had a great deal of luck hiding my emotions—especially those that betrayed my annoyance to certain things.

So either this guy was fucking stupid or he was just plain obtuse.

Either way, it pissed me the fuck off.

"Where were the guns taken to?" I asked, leaning my hip onto the metal table bolted to the floor.

He shifted slightly in his chair, the chains around his wrists clanking together as he did so. He was hooked up to a metal arm protruding out of the middle of the table, his handcuffs locking him in nice and secure.

Honestly, it kind of reminded me of my night with Max.

Hm. Probably not the best time to be thinking about that, I reminded myself.

"What the fuck...?" He turned his head slowly back toward me. "You think you can just slap me, you bi—"

I cracked him right across the face again.

I really didn't have the fucking time for this. He was lucky I wasn't already pulling out the switchblade I kept strapped to my thigh at all times. I bet he'd look real nice with a few less fingers.

"Where are the guns?" I bit out. "I want a location and name of who the fuck took them."

He scoffed. "I'm not giving you that information. You working with the cartel?"

I didn't answer him and instead crossed my arms over my chest. Typically, if I stayed staring a man down long enough, they folded quite easily. It wasn't often that men like him ever encountered a woman like me. Especially when he was already so vulnerable chained to a fucking table.

I had all the power here, and he knew it. His eyes darting around the room nervously told me as much.

"Look," he said after a long minute of silence. "I don't know what this is, but I'm not going to—"

I raised my hand again, feeling satisfied when he flinched back.

"Stop! Fuck, you've got a fucking man-hand. You know that?"

I lifted my other hand, giving him a nice show of the rings sitting nicely on my fingers. "Want to try this one? I was going easy on you earlier."

He frowned. "Listen. I don't—"

This time, I backhanded him, making sure to let my rings connect and drag right across the soft skin of his cheek. He let out a howl, his back arching in his chair as he tried to rip himself away from the handcuffs holding him in place. Thin lines of blood leaked down his cheek from where the prongs on my rings had caught against his skin.

"Fuck!! Fuck! What the fuck, you bitch!!"

"Tell me what I want to know. This is child's play to me. So if you want to keep all of your limbs intact and simply walk out of here with a little bit of bruising on your face, I suggest you start talking."

"I don't fucking know!" he yelled, his cheeks red. "I don't know where they got taken to! All I know is that we were ordered to take them, so we did!"

"By who?" I asked.

"My boss! Who the fuck do you think?"

That had me rolling my eyes and lifting my hand

once more. This time, though, I didn't slap him. Instead, I grabbed onto my switchblade and unhooked it from my thigh holster.

His eyes tracked me as I flipped it open. "What... what are you...?"

"You want to talk?" I held it up, letting the metal glint in the overhead light.

"I-I want a lawyer."

"Too late for that." I moved it around in my hand until the blade was facing downward.

"I want a lawyer! Who the fuck are you, a cop?! I've never seen a cop do this kind of interrogation before."

Whoever hired this guy was a fucking joke.

Using the force of my arm shifted upward, I plunged the knife down, stabbing him right through the back of his hand. The tip of the blade scratched against the metal table, making an awful noise that was cut off as the associate screamed in pain.

"Fuck!! Fuck!" He wiggled in his chair while his fingers flexed wildly, only furthering the damage the blade was doing as his tendons scraped against the sharp edge.

"Tell me what I want to know," I demanded.

I was done playing fucking games.

"T-The Machiavellis!" the man screamed. "That's who hired us!"

Well, well. So the pig's finally squealed.

"When?" I twisted it just enough for him to

scream again. "Do you work for them directly or do they just hire you for the bitch work?"

He writhed in pain. "Both!"

Interesting.

While I was taken a little aback by the revelation, I supposed I shouldn't be surprised. With Max and the Machiavelli heir showing up at my doorstep like they had, none of this could be considered a coincidence. Clearly, they'd been sent as a distraction while the real job had been to steal all my fucking product.

I should've shot Max after I fucked him.

My only regret about this whole thing, really.

Well, actually that wasn't exactly true. My only regret was not fucking him at the estate and *then* shooting him. I could've at least gotten off one last time on that cock of his before I took him out for good.

But I hadn't had the heart to at the time.

My gut instincts were rarely wrong, so this was more a surprise than anything. Usually I could sense a man's motives the second I locked eyes with him. But Max had been different. He'd drawn me in with his easy words, that body of his, and had made me believe he was just some bodyguard for the heir to some syndicate that I didn't care about.

Though who knew? Maybe he really was just that and he'd gotten himself caught up in all of this without meaning to. Regardless, he was going to die either way —unfortunately, really.

I needed to take out that entire family or else I'd regret it in the future.

I didn't need a syndicate walking around thinking that they could take whatever they wanted without consequences. That wasn't how the rules worked in these games. There were always repercussions to every action—an equal exchange of sorts.

That's what kept us all in balance with each other and kept those that thought to take control in line along with the rest of us.

Anyone who sought to step out of the natural order was soon reminded of why it was put in place in the first place.

And I would have absolutely no problem dishing out that sort of punishment.

I was owed that much, after all, for the trouble this was causing.

I drew my switchblade back, wiping the blood off on the man's shirt before snapping it closed again. He cowered away from me, the blood from his wound pooling down onto the table around it.

Pulling out my phone, I headed back to the door, banging my fist on it to be let out. When Dante answered the other line, I barked out a short.

"Get me the address to the Machiavelli compound."

"Yes, ma'am."

CHAPTER 9

Max

As it turned out, the guns were in fact stolen.

Not that it was any stretch of the imagination, but the fact that Senior had become this... well, desperate to recoup his losses over the diamond incident was something I never was expecting.

He'd been cagey when Ricard had asked him how in the world he'd procured such a large shipment of unregistered and unserialized guns in the two days we'd been gone. It'd set off alarm bells inside of my head the second the older man's eyes shifted away, a guilty look if I ever fucking saw one.

He'd spun the tale that the associates had been crossing the borders back from Arizona when they'd stopped in a small town called Boulder City for the night. Apparently, they'd met some kind of cartel there and had gotten into a fight with them, which resulted in both groups getting kicked out of the bar they'd both been loitering in.

It didn't take a genius to guess that with alcohol fueling their system along with pent-up testosterone rage, it'd boiled over to escalating into something that had ended with bodies on their hands.

According to Senior's recounting of the events, though, to me it sounded like much more than that.

If those guns had indeed come from a cartel, then the story of them fighting outside of the bar was simply underselling it. I'd had half a mind to call it out in the moment but had kept mouth shut as Ricard had pressed for more details.

His father didn't have much else to say after that, but it was clear that whatever had happened, there was a lot more to the story than what was being let on. Why Senior was trying to hide the truth from his own son was beyond me. It's not like the kid had a light stomach.

Hell, even with his father not knowing half the shit we were doing in the shadows, it was clear to anyone with a pair of eyes that the kid had matured over the last few months. He wasn't the same brat that jumped at the sound of something loud dropping or the click of a casing hitting the floor after a round was fired off.

Ricard had toughened up, and even to an absent father like Senior himself, that was clear to see.

Regardless of any of that, though, now we had an even bigger problem on our hands. With Senior getting stupid enough to wind up on the bad side of the cartel by stealing their guns, that meant sooner or later it would be tracked back down to this very estate.

No matter how well you tried to cover your tracks with selling this kind of shit, there was always a way of tracing it back to the source—that's what made the cartels a necessary third party in the first place.

If they wanted to sell you something, there were always strings attached. And Senior had not only stolen all of their shit, but he was planning on selling it to whoever the highest bidder happened to be.

Recouping his losses and then some from the looks of it.

But regardless of how many hands these guns were about to be passed through, eventually it was going to wind up with a big fat arrow pointing right back at him.

What a fucking dumbass.

Guns were a serious market and not for the faint of heart. That shit was as likely to get you killed as much as drug dealing was. Too many people would be vying for Senior's downfall, and like fuck I was about to let Junior go down with him. He could bitch and moan all he wanted about his son joining him in this business venture, but I wasn't about to let my boy get wrapped up in some dangerous shit like this when we already had our sights set on bigger and better things.

Dealing with the cartels had too many opportunities for failure that I simply wasn't willing to risk.

Not at this stage or any other in the future. If you wanted to walk away with less fingers and a few more bullet holes blown through your body, then by all means. But I for one was content with keeping my physical form intact, thank you very much.

As of a few days ago, I'd tasked Ricard with trying to get in touch with whatever cartel the guns had originally been taken from. Seeing as we'd only been gone for a few days, they were most likely local or had been passing through to get to whatever deal they were supposed to be delivering this amount of supply to.

However, it had soon come in through the grapevine that not only had the entire crew that had been transporting them in the first place had been slaughtered, but also that their actual bosses were nowhere to be found.

Not to mention there wasn't any word from disgruntled buyers, either.

While that sounded like some sort of dream come true that no one had come knocking on the front door of the estate, demanding their shit back, it also meant that there was a very real possibility that Senior had unknowingly gotten himself starting a war.

Cause whoever the fuck these belonged to was into some serious money. It had to be worth at least a million or more. There was too much stock for this to be some kind of amateur deal. Not to mention the care that had gone into concealing the serial numbers and keeping them out of the free market in order to sell on the black one.

All of this was getting way too out of hand.

By the end of the week, I was fucking beat.

I had no idea where to go from here. On the one

hand, I could just take Ricard and go—where, I didn't have a clue, but it was better than leaving us sitting here like fucking ducks.

On the other hand, that ran us the risk of being tracked down by not only Senior's people, but the cartel that most likely had marked us by this point as part of the fucking problem. Being associated in any way with Senior had fucked us over real good and was going to make it that much more difficult in getting out of this with both of our heads still attached to our bodies.

I need a fucking drink after all of this.

That was my first thought the second I'd parted ways with Ricard and had headed back to my apartment on the other side of the estate.

Blowing off some steam didn't sound half bad, especially when I was potentially staring down the end of a gun's barrel fairly soon.

Maybe getting a few drinks in me would help clear my head from all the fog clouding it. I wasn't usually one for anxiety, but then again, I normally had Caleb here to talk me down from the fucking ledge. Would it be absolutely stupid of me to do something impulsive and reckless as to kidnap Ricard? Yeah, of course. But that didn't stop the thought from running through my head over and over again until it made me dizzy.

When the fuck I'd gotten so attached to him, I had no clue. But the thought of letting him be taken down by the goodman cartel because of his old man pissed me off.

We needed an exit plan. And a good one if we were going to go down that route.

Stopping by my apartment first before heading out to the bar, I showered and got dressed in something a little more comfortable while also sneaking my gun under my clothes. There was no telling if we were already being watched, so I wasn't taking any chances of being nabbed off the streets like Caleb had been.

That was the kind of shit I never wanted to go through again.

If him staying down in Bali meant he would be safe for the rest of our days, then so be it. I could handle being separated.

Getting to the bar just after the sunset made for prime-time busyness on the streets down along the strip. I didn't normally like to come this way, much preferring the bars that were off the beaten path and had more locals than tourists. But I had a feeling that being out in the public eye like this was going to be less of a risk than putting myself in potentially isolating situations.

As long as I had a lot of eyes on me, I wasn't likely to be chloroformed and shoved into the back of some fucking van idling on the sidewalk.

The bar I'd chosen was crowded as all hell, but at least I knew that this place didn't charge out the ass for watered-down drinks catered to unsuspecting tourists. Loud talking filled the majority of the space, blocking out most of the music playing overhead—some techno beat that I could easily tune out.

I tossed a few bills onto the bar to wave the bartender over, catching his attention immediately.

"Give me whatever you've got on tap," I told him.

He nodded, shoving the bills into his front apron before heading off to grab a glass. My eyes tracked him as he moved to the other end of the bar. It wasn't until I caught sight of something familiar that it had me completely freezing in surprise.

There, at the other end of the bar, seated on one of the stools crammed between two college-looking girls, was Aylin.

No.

Fucking.

Way.

It was like deja vu all over again.

Pushing back through the throngs of people trying to climb over me to get their own orders in, I headed over to her. She was like a damn siren, calling to me without even knowing she was doing so. I doubted she even knew I'd spotted her. She'd had her attention on the two girls next to her, giving them both a sour face while a martini glass was clutched in her hand half empty.

What the hell is she doing all the way out here?

For a split second, I stopped in my tracks again.

The guns.

That couldn't be a coincidence, could it?

Gioni had asked Ricard to pick up a job with the cartel after all. And Senior had said he'd procured his shipment from the cartel. It only took two brain cells to put two-and-two together.

Fuck. She had to be here to gather info on what happened. Putting feelers out to see what hands the guns were going to be exchanged between. It was only logical to assume that, anyway. And I wasn't a damn fool to think that her showing up here four days after Senior's stunt was anything but planned.

Now, the real question was if she, or any of the Rosettis, suspected the Machiavellis of being the ones behind the transgressions. There were plenty of other mafia families within the surrounding area of both Nevada and Arizona that could potentially catch Aylin's eye before ours did. But that didn't guarantee that we were off the hook by any means.

Though that could be something to play into: act innocent and feed her false information to throw her and the rest of her syndicate off the trail. Not only would it give me an advantage of seeing just how much she knew or would let on, but I could also gauge how angry the Rosettis—and Gioni, more importantly— were regarding all of this.

It wasn't a foolproof plan, but it was the only thing I had at the moment.

Pushing through the crowds of people, I got over to her side of the bar and settled in on the opposite side of the college girls.

When the bartender came over and set my drink down in front of me, I let our arms brush together, catching her attention. She turned to me, those perfect lips of hers parting to, presumably, tell me off by the looks of it.

Her eyes widened when she caught sight of me.

"Max?"

I smirked. God, she was fucking good at playing up the act. I had to hand it to her. She should win an Oscar.

My cock jumped in my pants at that slow smile. I wondered what it'd feel like wrapped around me.

Here's the thing. I could always tell when someone was bullshitting me, even if they were a master at it. I just had that gut instinct in me that I treated like a lie detector. Was it infallible? No. But it often gave me a good sense to know when someone was trying to pull the wool over my eyes.

And right now, my bullshit meter was ring-a-linging.

"Fancy seeing you here," I drawled, grabbing my beer and taking a long swing of it. "Long way from Chicago, huh."

Was I being very subtle? Nah, but I wasn't going to treat Aylin like she was stupid. As much as she wanted me to believe that she was just some nobody, I couldn't let myself fall into the honey trap. It was too easy—too obvious. She deserved better than that of me just believing she was some glorified secretary with no stakes in the game.

Whatever leash she had the Rosetti family on, I hoped it was fucking tight. Because I could picture her sitting on a goddamn golden throne one day.

My pants tightened as my cock pressed up against my fly. Damn, a woman in power. Who knew that was my secret kink?

Aylin laughed a little, swirling the contents of her martini in her hand while the two college girls on the other side of her did a round of shots.

"Yeah, I've been all over the west, actually. My boss sent me over here."

"Oh really?" I pretended to care while listening to her lie, letting my eyes rake over her incredible body. "Weird they'd send someone like you."

Something flashed in her eyes at my words. I'd hit a nerve, apparently.

She quickly covered it up with a quick smile. "He trusts me to get the job done right."

God, I fucking want her so damn bad.

In a weird second of desperation to know, I almost let myself ask her how the hell she was dealing with being under Gioni's thumb. His temperament couldn't be easy to deal with. Not with Aylin's own *real* personality, not this fake one, was the complete polar opposite.

How could she deal with a guy like that as a boss?

She couldn't be that desperate for money, could she?

A twist in my gut had me almost letting myself blurt out something as equally stupid as my first held-back question: ditch the Rosettis and come work with me.

I at least would treat her with respect. She

wouldn't have to hide behind this weird... fake persona she was masking her true personality under to seem less like a shark among the school of fish she was wading through.

She could be her true self. That real Aylin that I mean back in the east where she'd been all play and all bite and left me completely vulnerable to her mercy.

That was the Aylin I wanted to see again. Not this watered-down version.

Maybe I was getting ahead of myself.

"Max." Her voice broke me out of my thoughts.

"Yes?"

She flashed me a smile—the same one that she had weeks ago that promised all the kinds of pain and pleasure that heaven and hell could offer.

"Want to get out of here with me?"

Oh fuck yes I did.

Screw feeding her false information. I could do that after we were both panting and left satisfied staring at the ceiling while we tried to steady our heart rates.

I turned toward the bar, downing the rest of my beer in a few deep pulls before setting the glass back down onto it and standing.

"Shall we?"

CHAPTER 10

Aylin

BRINGING Max back to my hotel room was both planned and an astronomically stupid idea on my part.

I'd had every intention of kidnapping him the second I'd noticed him wandering into the bar—my fingers already halfway to typing out a message to my associates to bring our car around so that our exit could be smooth and seamless as we shoved him into the trunk. It would've been easy too—he looked not only tired but lost in thought as he'd sat down and ordered himself a drink.

But as soon as he'd come around and sat down next to me, I felt that familiar pull aching in my belly. The want to have him under me, begging for me to let him cum as I rode him until his eyes rolled into the back of his head.

It was too loud to ignore.

I could control this situation. I just needed to be diligent and not let myself get lost in Max's overly flirtatious charm like I'd been tempted to back at my family's estate.

Which... was easier said than done. Especially when the second we got to my hotel room, he grabbed me by the waist and lifted me clear off my feet in order to press me against the wall right inside of the doorway.

I grabbed onto the back of his hair and slammed our lips together, both of our mouths parting instantly to tangle our tongues. It was an erotic display of all the pent-up frustration I'd been feeling since all of this had begun almost six weeks ago.

Max had never been something I'd expected. He was an outlier that had come crashing through the carefully constructed equation and had managed to bulldoze his way right in the middle of my path. Never in my life had I been so turned on by a man before— wanted him badly enough to take him to bed twice.

Yet here I was, pushing Max back as I demanded, "Bed. Now."

My voice was already breathy sounding from our kiss. Barely anything had happened between us, and I was already set to come undone.

What was this man doing to me?

Max peeled me away from the wall, walking us with his arms propped up under my ass to keep me pressed against his chest as he headed over to the bed. My legs tightened around his waist, anticipation curling in my gut and making it harder for my more rational thoughts to take route.

My body was piloting my brain. My wants and desires took the forefront of my head space and made it difficult to remain objective even as he tossed me down onto the bed and crawled on top of me.

My hand reached out to grab at his shirt, pulling him down into another bruising kiss. It wasn't often that I let myself do this—give in to my carnal pleasures without some other ulterior motive attached to it that led me down this path in the first place.

I would absolutely be interrogating Max after this, but for now, I could enjoy the ride and let myself go just this once.

His hands snuck down my waist, teasing the skin exposed where my pants and shirt met. His fingers curled up under my top, pushing it up as he drew his hands closer to my chest. I bit his tongue the second he had a hold of my breasts and inwardly laughed to myself when he instantly pulled back.

I smiled up at him. "What, don't like a little bit of pain?"

"Oh, is that what that was?" He grinned, replacing his hands back over my bra. "And here I thought you were objecting."

"If I was, you'd know it."

Hooking my leg around his waist once more, I pushed up against his chest with a firm jab, catching him off guard enough to roll us over. As soon as his back hit the mattress, I crawled on top of him, straddling him before sitting down directly over his crotch.

He groaned at the pressure of my hips on his,

rolling them slightly under me to grind his cock against my ass.

"Fuck..."

"So desperate." I smirked, pushing his shirt up to reveal his abs. "Don't tell me you waited around to get laid."

He let out a breathy chuckle, his stomach constricting from the movement and outlining those hard muscles under his skin. "Sounds a bit romantic, doesn't it?"

I let my brow shoot up. "What, you waiting around for the chance to fuck me again? Didn't take you as the kind of man to fall so easily."

"Don't sell yourself short."

While his words were said in a teasing tone, I couldn't help myself by reading into them. I doubted Max meant anything behind it, let alone telling me so upfront that he was falling for me. It wasn't like we knew each other outside of this strange arrangement we've found ourselves in. And he had to be stupid not to assume I was here looking for the guns his fucking boss took.

If he was that obtuse, I'd be disappointed. For all the cunning intelligence that I suspected lay right beneath the surface of those flashy smiles, I didn't want it to be all for show. Even as enemies, it made for a more interesting opponent.

Pushing that back from my mind, I tugged at his shirt until he lifted himself off the mattress and allowed me to pull it up over his head. I tossed it away from me, my hands automatically coming down to trace along his flushed skin and small pucker marks from old wounds.

I was curious for the stories behind them all. Max didn't strike me as the type to unnecessarily get himself into danger, let alone get stabbed and shot this many times by the looks of it. Of course, being in the military I was sure had been the kind of job to force him to get down and dirty every once in a while, but not this much.

My fingers pressed against what looked like an old burn mark—small in size and rounder than I was expecting.

Cigarette burn?

Interesting.

He grabbed my wrist, pulling my hand away from his skin. "As much as I love you admiring my beauty, I would like to get you naked."

"Eager," I chastised him but tugged my own shirt and bra off of my body anyway.

I was just as raring to go to get this show on the road as he was. However, I was much better at hiding it.

I had to bite the inside of my cheek when he pinched one of my nipples between two of his fingers, rolling the bud gently before applying just enough pressure that a moan came rolling out of me. Fuck, if I wasn't a sucker for a little pain that came with my pleasure. That was the kind of high that was hard to chase after and do well, but so far, Max had been continually surprising me. So maybe this wouldn't be a complete disappointment like all the others I'd taken to bed before him.

Our first time had been all about me. I'd taken what I'd wanted and left him to deal with the consequences. It had been satisfying for sure to watch him struggle with his handcuffs as I left, his cock hard and desperate to get me back around him until he could cum properly.

However, this time around I wanted it all. I wanted him to fuck me until we were both seeing stars. I wanted us to forget our damn names and why we were both in this city in the first place. There was nothing else here to worry about other than getting each other off so good that we'd be thinking about it for days to come.

Max surprised me yet again by rolling us back over and pining me to the bed. His mouth descended onto my body, leaving a trail of open-mouthed kisses along the column of my neck and down to my chest before he wrapped his lips around one of my nipples.

I groaned again, feeling my hips kick up and meet his.

As much as I loved foreplay, I really needed him to fuck me.

Grabbed at the back of his hair, I yanked him back and held him until his eyes fluttered open. He blinked at me with those gray eyes, wonder and lust making his pupils blown out.

"Pants off. Now."

He licked his lips. "I'm not done."

I tightened my grip. "I don't care."

He let out a soft growl, his Adam's apple bobbing as he swallowed.

I didn't know why it never occurred to me before this, but the man seemed to like taking orders. Which was obvious considering his background. He'd been taking orders from higher-ups presumably his entire adult life. So of course he'd find it erotic to do so in bed with someone like me under him.

I let him go, giving him the room to sit back and grab onto the waistband of my tailored pants. They were an expensive material that right now I couldn't for the life of me care about getting wrinkled. Reaching down, I unhooked my switchblade from one of the belt loops and tossed it onto the bed next to me within arms' reach.

Max barely glanced over at it—much too entranced with what he was doing.

His fingers hooked under them on either side of my hips, sliding together until they were both at the button.

He popped it apart, parting my pants before slowly sliding them down over my hips and thighs, my underwear going with it.

I let my legs fall open as he stripped me, giving him a full view of my wet pussy.

"Jesus." His fingers dug into the meat of my thighs, prying my legs further apart. "I want to taste you so bad."

"Later," I told him, nodding to the bulge hidden under his own pants. "Off."

"Yes, ma'am." He smirked.

Sitting back again, he shoved his pants down his thighs, his cock popping free and giving me a full show as he struggled to kick them off. I pushed up onto my elbow, reaching out with my free hand to grab a hold of him, to feel that thick, hot length weighted in my hands.

He groaned the second I tightened my fingers around him, letting me lead him like a fucking dog on a leash as I tugged him closer using the base of his cock.

"Come here," I told him, letting my arm move out from under me so I could fall back down onto the mattress.

I brought my hips back, giving him enough room to settle between my legs as I lined the head of his cock up against my entrance. I was already wet enough that he had no problem sliding right in, burying himself until our hips were pressed flushed together.

I flexed my walls around him, clenching down on that thick length that had my stretched wide open. Every part of me could feel him perfectly. The veins along his cock practically imprinting themselves to the inside of me like some kind of remembrance.

Fuck, I'd missed this.

He rocked into me, leaning over until he had both hands resting on either side of my head to hold himself up. I grabbed onto his waist in order to move against him to meet the pumping of his hips that soon turned into hard thrusts.

Our hips smacked together, over and over again. I could feel my own slick wetting the bed under me. I hadn't realized how pent up I'd been until I'd decided to take him back to my hotel room with me. And even then, this was rather ridiculous.

How could a man make me so fucking horny that I was losing all pieces of myself? It seemed impossible, given that I never would've let myself get to this point in the first place with anyone else.

But Max, it seemed, was different.

I wanted to chastise myself with the thought.

I felt his breath panting over me, his head coming down to rest against mine as he drove into me. With each roll of his hips, he pressed hard against me, rubbing my clit just enough that it was teasing me into the edges of an orgasm.

Reaching down between us, my fingers found the sensitive bud. I rolled it between my pointer and middle finger, circling it faster and faster as Max began to lose himself in fucking me.

When my orgasm hit, I moaned against his mouth.

Pleasure curled at the base of my spine, spreading up to the rest of my body and blooming outward. It was enough to make my toes curl and my thighs snap against his waist from the pressure.

"Fuck," he breathed out.

I pressed up against his chest suddenly. "Up."

"No way you're doing this to me again," he growled.

I wanted to laugh the second his hand reached up to grab at one of my wrists in order to pin it to the bed.

"Up," I told him again, slapping his hand away.

"Aylin—"

I shoved at his chest once more. "Roll over, you fucking oaf."

Just like the good boy he was, he did as he was told, taking me with him in the process. I smiled down at him as I settled on top of him, taking in the actual pout that was tugging his mouth down.

"Who knew I could render someone like you to this state?" The tease came as natural as breathing to me.

His fingers tightened around my hips, holding me in place so as to not let me get up off him. Really, it was sort of charming that he thought I'd be *that* cruel and leave him with blue balls twice in a row.

Well... I guess considering myself, it wasn't that much of a stretch.

I rocked against him, resting my hands on his abs to keep me upright. At his gasp, I tilted my head back, letting my hair fall back behind me while my eyes closed.

"I could go for round two," I told him.

"Fuck yes, you can," he encouraged.

Riding him felt even better. At this angle, I could rub my clit against him with each movement of my hips. He was deep enough inside me that I could feel the head of his cock brushing up against my cervix with each pass. The slight pinch of pain felt good against the almost unbreakable wall of pleasure I was high on.

"Aylin," he called out, squirming under me. "Jesus. You look so good up there."

Damn right I did.

My tits bounced as I got more into it. Max's fingers tightened on my hips, helping me with how far I could get my body up before slamming right back down onto him.

Shit, I was already feeling another orgasm tingling up my spine.

"Fuck. I'm close," he said.

At his words, my walls clenched around him again.

"Shit," he huffed out, his spine practically arching right off the bed to get as deep as he could into me.

I felt his cum spill into me, coating me from the inside and giving me just enough of a push to fall over the edge again. I slammed back down on him and let myself rest there, my pussy contracting over and over as it tried milking his cock for everything that it had.

Max groaned again, flexing his fingers to dig into my skin. "Oh my god..."

His voice sounded strained as he continued to cum. It was perfect.

When both of our bodies finally relented, I leaned heavily on my arms to keep myself upright. It'd been a long time since I'd been fucked like this and had felt so satisfied afterward.

Too bad I couldn't steal him to take him back to Chicago with me. He'd make a wonderful pet.

I opened my eyes slowly to look down at him. His hands fell away from where they'd been holding onto me, dropping down uselessly on either side of him.

He was staring up at me, his chest rising and falling rapidly as he caught his breath.

"Damn," he finally mumbled.

Honestly, I felt the same way.

Before he could move me off of him, I tightened my thighs around his waist again and slowly leaned over to reach for the switchblade I'd tossed earlier. He didn't stop me, much too busy still coming down from his high to slap the blade out of my hand before I could retract it.

The second I flipped it open, he blinked at me. His chuckle was breathy as he stared at the knife pointed at his neck.

"Robbing me? Come on, Aylin. I thought we were past this."

I swiped a few strands of hair away from my sweaty face, my heart still hammering inside of my chest. I could feel his cum slightly leaking out of me as I shifted our hips to get more comfortable, earning myself another moan from him.

"Where are the guns, Max?"

CHAPTER 11

Max

MAYBE THERE WAS something seriously wrong with me, but being held up at knifepoint while still inside of her was more of a turn-on than I would've given myself credit for having.

"Max." She narrowed her eyes at me when my dick twitched.

"Would you believe me if I told you I have no idea what you're talking about?"

"No."

Welp. At least I gave it the old college try.

"So…" I tried to stall for time. "Your boss sent you here…"

"We already went over this. Where are the guns?" The cool metal of the steel against my flushed chest surprised me with how unpleasant it felt.

I snorted. "You fuck me and then you threaten me. Come on, Aylin. Where's the romance?"

I could tell she was fighting a smile by the way her

lips twitched slightly. Her finger flexed around the hilt of her switchblade, the movement causing her tendon to move under the thin skin of her hand. It was a weirdly erotic sort of gesture that had me staring. If I hadn't cum already, I certainly would've at the sight of that.

She had nice hands.

"Look. I can't really confirm or deny any knowledge about what you're talking about," I told her.

Her eyes narrowed again.

"But," I held up my hands, trying to give her the impression of solidarity, "I can give you something else."

I didn't want this to be some kind of strife between our families. Or rather, her and Ricard's family since I wasn't anything more than just a third party at this point.

Not before I could get him out of there.

If her boss and Senior wanted to go at it after we were gone, then that was their fucking business. I wouldn't stop them.

"I'm not interested in negotiations," she said, her hand not wavering in the slightest.

"What if it got your boss his guns back?"

That caught her attention.

Her fingers flexed again. "Go on."

I wasn't a fool to think I had her just yet. Aylin wasn't the type to easily fall for charmed words and a thinly veiled promise. She demanded results, and if I couldn't deliver them... well, I'd soon find that knife jabbed right through my jugular.

"Look. I know of an auction happening in a few days." The words were coming out of my mouth before I had time to properly think them over. "Your guns might be among them, I don't know. But I can get you in."

"Where's this auction happening?"

Shit. Of course she would ask that.

To tell the truth, I had no fucking clue what I was saying. I was making this shit up as I went. But it sounded good enough to be believable. I needed Aylin to get her sights off the Machiavellis before she called up Gioni and sicced his fucking dogs on us.

"I don't have all the details. But like I said, I can get you in. We can work together on this."

She huffed out a laugh. "I don't work with lap dogs."

Ouch.

Though point taken.

"You want your boss' guns back, this is the only solution."

Her eyes narrowed. "Really? And what if I just leave your body on the stoop of the Machiavellis' estate? What then?"

Even with her light tone, I knew she was dead serious. There was no one on this planet that couldn't see the deadly look in her eyes that made those pretty light irises darken until they looked almost black. On top of me like this, with a knife to my throat and looking ever the viper that I knew she was.

"Nothing, really." I shrugged. "I'm just a lap dog, remember? They'll replace me in a day."

As sad as it was, it was the truth. I doubted anyone but Caleb—and maybe Sam by extension—would ever mourn me if I was wiped off the face of the planet.

He'd probably want to seek revenge or whatever, and I was sure Sam would have to talk him down from it, telling him something along the lines of, "This wouldn't be what Max wanted," or whatever the fuck nonsense she liked to spout to keep him clean from his assassin days.

Though here was the thing about that in general: it wasn't like Caleb would be notified right away if I died anyway.

He had no relationship with Senior at all after ditching him for New York. And I doubted Ricard would be kind enough to call him up to tell him the news.

I mean, maybe he would. Who knew? That kid was constantly surprising me. But he and Caleb had always had a weirdly adverse relationship that I was sure was partially fueled by me in some way.

As flattering as it was to have them fighting over me, sometimes it got rather fucking annoying to say the least.

Blinking myself out of my thoughts, I focused back on Aylin when she shifted her weight on me again. She was frowning—an expression that genuinely surprised me. She'd lowered the knife from my throat and let her forearm rest on top of her thigh. She still had the blade open and pointed at me, giving me absolutely no room to do something stupid like make a fast move on her.

I'd sooner find that blade going right through my hand before I could get a chance to grab it from her. Especially at this angle.

I could tell she wanted to say something after my confession, but she couldn't quite get the words out.

Which was odd since she always had something to say.

Was it all that surprising that my job was easily replaced? Honestly, I was probably their longest standing bodyguard yet, and that was only because I'd made myself useful and also wasn't a fucking idiot.

"Aylin." I sighed. "We can work together on this."

I didn't want us to be adversaries on this. It was easier if we worked together to get what she wanted. I didn't want the guns just as much as she *wanted* them. The math was simple.

"Why did you take my guns?" she asked.

I frowned. "I didn't. I had nothing to do with any of that. Though, now that we're on the topic, why is it that your boss was careless enough to lose that much product?"

Her lips thinned.

I really was great at digging my own grave, especially by insulting her employer so blatantly. Back when I was growing up, I'd often find myself being told that I had "foot-in-mouth" syndrome. It wasn't until years later and a few slaps across the cheek that I'd been clued into what exactly that meant.

This would most definitely be one of those times.

My impulsive mouth really knew no bounds.

"You think it's wise to be a smartass right now?" she asked.

"Unfortunately, it's chronic," I shot back at her. "Most would classify it as a disease at this point."

"Max," she grit out through her teeth. "I'm not playing games. If you're actually serious about getting my supply back, then fine. But if I find out that you're trying to fuck me over on this, you're going to wish I put this knife in your throat. That would be much more merciful than what I have in mind for you if you betray me."

I nodded slowly. "Of course."

"Good."

Clipping her knife back had me breathing out a sigh of relief that I didn't know I'd been holding this entire time. When Aylin rolled herself to her feet, my dick slid out her, falling back down onto my belly limp and still wet from all of our fluids.

She hopped off the bed and gathered my clothes off of the floor before tossing them to me.

"Now get the fuck out."

CHAPTER 12
Ricard

AS MUCH AS I hated to bend to my father's will, there were some things that I still had a hard time treading the line with when it came to his undue wrath.

While my father was a smart businessman, he also had a quick temper that never seemed to stop short in making me question whether or not it was worth getting on his bad side about.

This morning, I'd been woken up early by Max banging on my door, telling me that we'd needed to talk. Bleary eyed and barely awake, I'd let him in and settled down onto one of my couches as he rattled off about some plan in getting my father to agree to host an auction off property for the weapons in the vault.

At first, I had no clue what the fuck he was talking about.

Apparently, he'd met some woman who turned out to be the assistant to none other than Gioni

Rosetti himself. While it wasn't surprising that any of this shit had Gioni's name stamped on it, what did have me raising my brow at Max was the fact that that brat had sent a woman to locate this amount of valuable product.

While I never cared for the whole boys' club—seeing as my own mother practically held the marionette strings to my father's empire—that didn't mean that everyone else had that kind of new-aged thinking.

Gioni Rosetti struck me as the type of person to never let a woman infiltrate the upper ranks. At least none that would be dealing with such large exchanges of money. It was also hard to believe that he'd send one woman instead of an entire team to track down who the fuck had procured the shipment right out from their own noses.

But for some reason, Max seemed convinced that this was the real deal. He always talked about having the gut feeling, and while I honestly wanted to argue against it, it really had never steered us wrong.

Which brought me to where I was headed to today: tasked with convincing my father to not only host an auction for the weapons in order to get this woman Max knew through the venue doors, but for the entire event to be held off property.

My father tended to be an overly paranoid person. So getting him to agree to doing this out of her territory, a place he could control with complete certainty, was going to be a task in of itself.

Blowing out a breath, I stopped in front of his office door and rattled my knuckles against it.

Max had coached me all morning. Going over line after line on how to spin this without one, looking insane and two, without looking suspicious of my own motives. My father was already suspicious of our random comings and goings but had yet to call it out.

Seeing as how he was too busy with his new business endeavor, it at least gave me a sort of advantage here. He wanted to make money, recoup his losses from my royal fuck-up. Well, where was a golden opportunity for that?

When the door to his office opened up, my second cousin Antoni appeared in the doorway. His salt-and-pepper hair was pushed back away from his face, making him look almost identical to his brother, my other second cousin, Vinny.

Their own defining difference was that one wore glasses and the other didn't.

I could remember many times when I couldn't tell the two apart when I was younger. Now, as they got older and so did I, the difference became a little more apparent.

"I need to speak with my father," I told him, keeping my shoulders rolled back and my head high.

Unfortunately, most of the people within the estate—including my own family and staff—still thought of me as the brat who couldn't be controlled. A mindset that typically got me heated because from that, I would constantly be babied.

I fucking hated it.

It was hard growing up in this kind of family as it was. I didn't need that shit piled on top of me too.

Antoni looked me up and down slowly, clearly displeased that I was here interrupting whatever was going on inside of my father's office. I really didn't care, though. I was still the heir to this family. I had just as much say in kicking people out as my father did.

"Ricard?" my father called over Antoni's shoulder.

I pushed past the man and headed through the doorway. "I need to speak with you."

He was at his desk, paperwork fanned out in front of him. As I grew closer, I glanced down at his desk, noticing that the paperwork actually seemed to be financial records. Next to one of the stacks was a wire basket filled with other papers, though these were different from the rest. On the top page, there was a long list of gun types that was followed by the retail price. Each line was individually colored, marked with a different highlighter.

Actually, that made my job much easier.

With my father already being overly meticulous with our finances since the incident, I knew he was desperate to get to selling those guns. He wanted to turn a profit to get back into whatever business schemes he had going on that I still wasn't privy to knowing.

Hopefully he'd be eager enough in his venture to listen to me.

I nodded to the pile. "Have you thought about holding an auction?"

He gave me a puzzled look. "For the sale?"

"Yes. You can invite enough people to start a bidding war. I'm sure there'll be enough interest to drive up the price."

He sat back in his chair, considering the information for a moment. I could see the gears working internally, analyzing my words, and he worked through all of the possibilities of this plan succeeding. While it wasn't exactly foolproof, Max had had a point when he'd brought it up to me originally: there was no way that an opportunity like this could be turned down, even if it was to see what happened.

No matter what, my father needed to sell these guns. He couldn't keep them collecting dust in the vault any longer than it took for our contacts to start calling us, asking for their loan paybacks. Which I was sure he'd more than likely already started receiving by now.

Even if the weapons were unsold at an undervalued price, it was more money in his pocket than he had before all of this started.

"We can invite some of our contacts," I offered when he remained silent in thought. "Maybe we can even get some of Liam Harrington's contacts to stop by. Might be a good opportunity to establish those connections again."

That had him lighting up almost instantly. "That's not a bad idea, son."

I smirked internally.

Hook, line, and sinker.

"I can get the word out about it," I offered.

My father shook his head. "No need. I'll be handling this. I want to keep this sale exclusive and not let word get out to anyone that can't afford what I'm charging."

I held back pointing out that by that logic, it wouldn't exactly be an auction then. But then again, I didn't exactly care how the hell my father got rid of his supply. So long as it was out our doors by the time the cartel came around knocking, that was.

I could tell that Max had been apprehensive this entire time over this situation. It wasn't like him to be so distraught, and that nervousness was also kind of rubbing off on me. We hadn't exactly talked about the whys on what his attitude shift was all about, but if it had anything to do with this woman and Gioni, then I supposed it was warranted.

No matter what, I knew Max was looking out for me and himself. Neither of us wanted to be dragged down with my father for his stupid decisions to get involved with the cartel—or, rather, *against* the cartel.

There was a part of me that felt bad for my mother, though. She'd be swept up whether she wanted to be or not. I guessed it was that little boy still inside of me that wanted to protect her from harm, even if she was most likely going to be just as much of a cause to it all as my father was.

I hadn't seen her since Max and I had gotten back

from Chicago, and while that was a typical occurrence, it still felt off.

With this entire gun-thing going on, where the hell could she be? I doubted she felt that this was a trivial matter and didn't warrant her attention.

"Let me know when it's going on," I said to my father, stepping back from his desk. "I want to be there when it's going on."

He was already waving a dismissive hand at me while getting up from his desk, the papers on it already long forgotten.

"Yes. Plan for this weekend."

I nodded and headed to the door. "Got it."

Max paced around my room.

"If it's going to be a closed-off event, how the hell am I going to get Aylin in there?"

I shrugged at him, my eyes tracking his movements. "I don't know. She doesn't have to be there, does she?"

"She needs to identify the product to make sure it's the Rosettis's."

I snorted and then lounged back into my couch. "I mean I feel like it's pretty obvious that it is. It can't be a coincidence that she's looking for an entire cache of guns and my father just so happened to steal some."

Max rolled his eyes, giving me a look over his

shoulder as he passed by me. "This really isn't the time for that, Ricard."

I hated when he scolded me. It brought me right back to when I was a kid and my father was yelling at me for something stupid. Not to mention, it wasn't like I was poking at him just for fun. Even if the guns turned out to not be Gioni's family's, who cared?

We needed them gone, and Gioni needed a supply back. It was a win-win in my book, if I was being honest.

This was the problem when it came to mafia families: there were too many arbitrary rules that literally didn't make any sense. As long as someone had something that someone else wanted, who cared about the details in between?

"If you're that bent out of shape about sneaking her in, then we can just take her in through the back. You're going to be there acting as my bodyguard anyway. I can keep my father distracted long enough for you to run off and go get her."

Max shook his head, pivoting in a smooth twist before heading in the opposite direction. "That's not what I'm worried about. It's your father seeing some random woman he doesn't recognize and calling it out. She's a good bluffer but in a room full of people who already know each other."

"Okay," I drawled. "Then I'll have my father invite Gioni."

Max stopped in his tracks, turning to me. "What, and have her come in his stead?"

I shrugged. "You said it yourself that she does all of their bitch work. Gioni's a fucking prick. Why wouldn't he get someone to do something like this for him?"

He nodded slowly, his eyes wandering off as he weighed the options in his head.

Honestly, this was the best plan we had. Not to mention that the event was planned for this weekend, which was only two days away. We didn't have time to come up with something elaborate. We needed to work with what we had and make fucking due.

"Let me run it by her and see what she thinks. It's her boss' call, not hers."

"Fine." I pushed myself up from the couch. "Just get me an answer by the end of the day. I need time to warm my father up to the idea so we can't be waiting around to hear back from her."

A slow smile worked its way onto Max's face. "Damn, Ricard. Look at you dishing out orders like you know what you're doing."

I flushed, both annoyed and flattered by the compliment. "Shut up. I just know my dad, all right? He's more of a prick than you."

Max winked at me. "Least I make things fun."

Sometimes, I would love to pull out my gun and shove it in his damn mouth to keep his lips from flapping.

Max laughed as if reading my mind. He crossed my room and then slung an arm around my shoulders, pulling me in for a tight side hug.

"I'll let you know in a few hours what she says. Sounds good."

I nodded, nudging him with my elbow. "The sooner we get this over with, the better."

"Agreed."

CHAPTER 13

Max

HEARING BACK from Aylin was both a blessing and a curse.

Ever since our little rendezvous at her hotel, I couldn't stop thinking about her. She completely consumed my thoughts every waking second and teased me at night every time I closed my eyes and tried to get some sleep—which I hadn't been able to do a lot of lately, given the circumstances.

She'd been down for our plan of getting her into the event, even going so far as to say that her boss' opinion on the subject didn't matter so long as she got to see the supply for herself and confirm that it was indeed theirs.

"He'll agree to whatever I tell him to," is what she'd told me over the phone. *"I want my fucking guns back."*

Her words, even if they were spoken with anger behind them, were so hot.

It was interesting to me the way she'd all but taken over ownership of this entire endeavor.

Whatever Gioni had said to her before she'd left Chicago to come here had clearly been stressing her out to the point where she felt personally responsible for getting this job down. Going so far as to think that the supply of guns was not only her boss' but hers too.

I could appreciate that in a woman.

It gave me the sense that in the future, I might be seeing more of Aylin running something. While I doubted she could go very far being a woman—unfortunate, considering she would be a force to be reckoned with—she could at least climb up to some rung of the proverbial ladder that gave her power.

That's where she belonged anyway.

Too bad Ricard didn't have his own syndicate yet. Or I'd have half a mind to suggest he partner up with her.

Though, then again, they both had the personality type of not wanting to share soooo, there was that.

By the time the weekend rolled around, we'd gotten word of the event taking place in a prestigious auction house a few blocks away from the strip. I had no idea what contacts Senior had managed to connect with and talk them into coming, but the place was buzzing when Ricard and I finally arrived Saturday night.

"Damn," Ricard muttered to me as we passed through the front entrance together. "Didn't think this many people were interested in the arms dealings."

I glanced around as our IDs were scanned into the system; the suit jacket I was wearing was a little too snug for my comfort and made it rather annoying to conceal my weapon under. Blessedly, there were no metal detectors that awaited us as we headed inside after collecting our IDs back from the bouncer at the front.

"You'd be surprised how many people want to break into that industry. Between that and drugs, it's a money maker."

Ricard snorted. "Yeah, I get that. But dealing with cartels? That's..."

I glanced over at him, smiling a little.

Actually, we'd never had this conversation before on what he wanted to do once he had his own syndicate. Obviously we needed a way to make easy cash the first year or two being out on our own, but after we had Ricard's name well established in the underground, then it was kind of fair game for anything.

While I agreed with him about the gun's thing and it being dangerous to deal with, I didn't exactly want to take it off the table entirely. If by some miracle we could survive this latest ordeal unscathed, then maybe it would give us a good in with the Rosetti family.

We were, after all, kind of saving their skin by getting their guns back without an all-out war.

That had to count for something.

Having to deal with Gioni again wasn't my flavor of ideal, but perhaps Aylin could climb up in the ranks enough after this that she would become our point of contact.

The idea sent a shiver up my spine.

I wouldn't mind that *at all*.

"It doesn't have to exclusively be with cartels," I finally said as we headed into the main ballroom. "We could be dealing with other groups like direct buyers or the government."

His head whipped around. "The *government*? Please tell me you're actually hearing yourself."

I rolled my eyes and swung my arm around to catch him into a loose headlock. "Relax. That's at least a few years away from now. Let's focus on tonight, okay?"

He relaxed under me, muttering a, "Yeah, yeah," before pulling away.

Atta boy.

We stopped inside of the ballroom where there had been chairs set up in uniform rows all facing a stage. With the amount of people that had shown up and were milling about, it was clear to me that Senior had somehow seen this as an opportunity for not just his own auction, but for one in general.

There were way too many people here that hardly looked like arms dealers or buyers for this to be just a simple viewing of the product he had and a quick sale to get it out of his vault.

Which, I was positive, he'd been talked into by someone outside of his circle. Because there was no fucking way Gianna would've approved of any of this.

Not that I'd seen her at all recently.

Odd, really. She was always up Senior's ass about stuff like this.

I pushed the thought away in order to shove my hand down into my slacks' pocket to retrieve my phone. I already had a few messages from Aylin waiting for me by the time I turned my phone back on. She'd been eager for updates—something I couldn't exactly blame her for.

I knew her boss was most likely breathing down her neck about this transaction going smoothly. The details on what she'd discussed with him were still unknown to me, as well as how in the fuck she was going to get a hold of the supply once she positively identified it as Rosetti property.

She'd told me not to worry about it and that it was being handled, but there was a slightly nagging feeling in my gut that I was having a hard time ignoring. Sure, I trusted that she had a plan, but would it work with how disillusioned Senior was acting?

The man had it in his head that tonight he was going to be on the verge of making millions. I doubted Gioni had giving the go-ahead to Aylin to spend that kind of cash on product that was literally there in the first place. So how the hell was any of this going to work?

It gave me a fucking migraine just thinking about it, honestly.

"I'm going to go catch up with my dad," Ricard

was saying to me. "Come find me when you and what's-her-face get ahold of each other."

I reached up and ruffled his hair, not being able to help myself. "Sure thing."

He batted my hand away from his before ducking away from me and heading out into the ballroom. I followed his direction, spotting Senior near the stage talking with a small group of men that I vaguely recognized.

There were plenty of people here that I knew if I concentrated enough, I could figure out who the fuck they were. Local syndicates along with some out-of-towners I was sure. Whatever else Senior was planning on presenting tonight would be of little interest to me —though I could use the downtime in between sales before Aylin's popped up in order to get an idea of which direction I could push Ricard in.

There were plenty of illegal activities up on the market that could make us money. We just had to get creative with it. And what better way to do that than by looking at other people's shit?

I headed out of the ballroom to a quieter part of the auction house. I still hadn't come up with a way to sneak Aylin in if she was turned away at the door, so I hoped like fuck that she was right about her boss having enough of a pull all the way in the west that would get her in here.

If not, then we were royally fucked. Because I highly doubted I was going to be allowed to take pictures to send to her.

Putting the phone up to my ear after dialing her number, it rang until the automated voicemail was picked up. Hm, that was odd. Usually, Aylin would answer right away—

"Max," a voice called to me from behind, causing me to spin around.

And there she was, dressed in a tight-fitting red gown that showed off every delicious inch of her, along with a large slit that practically exposed an entire hip. I had to bite the inside of my cheek to keep myself from grinning. This wouldn't be the most ideal time to come onto her, especially since I knew she was stressed out getting this job done.

The last thing I wanted to do was get in her way, even though that's what my entire brain was screaming at me to do.

What could I say? I was a simple man that liked it when the girl I was interested in was a little mean to me.

"Hey, you got in," I said, pocketing my phone.

She tucked a small clutch under her arm, nodding to me. Her long black hair was pulled back from her face with a braid that looped around the back of her head in a loose fit. There were a few strands of her hair that had escaped the styling and were hanging around her face.

Her eye makeup was dark and gave her a sultry look that had my cock hardening in my pants. Especially when she gave me a hard once-over.

I tucked my hands into my pockets. "Welcome to the shitshow."

I could tell she was fighting the urge to smirk at me, trying to remain as impassive as possible to my *very* charming wit. "Funny. They start the auction yet?"

"No. We got time to hang."

I let the word hover in the air. Hey, if she wanted to get down and dirty in the meantime to kill a few minutes, I was obviously ready. Maybe it was a bit tacky to want to be dragged off to a dingy supply closet, but again: I was a simple man.

Even though I wasn't expecting much, she in fact surprised me by taking the bait. "Oh really? And what exactly entails this 'hanging out'?"

Oh my god, was she actually going to let me drag her off into a broom closet and fuck her?

Judging by the way she was eyeing me closely, I'd say that was a big ol' fat *yes*.

Damn, I was a lucky son of a bitch.

Weaving my arm around her waist, I tugged her back into my chest, letting her breasts press up against me. She was warm, even through the material of her dress. Her eyes flitted up to look at me, those brown irises practically sucking all of the light out of the room.

Her tan skin was soft to the touch as I ran a hand up her exposed thigh where the slit in her dress was. She pushed her hands against my chest, forcing me to walk backward. "You're really going to start that out here?"

"No ma'am." I grinned. "I'd much rather have you all to myself."

"I'm surprised you don't like to show off."

"I do, but not with this." I grabbed her again, practically tugging her off her feet as I walked us further down the hallway and down an abandoned side section of the venue.

"And why's that?" she asked, looking up at me again.

I was surprised she was letting me manhandle her like this, though like fuck I was going to complain about it. I was lucky she was even willing to let me touch her after all of the stress she'd been under.

"Because I don't like the thought of sharing you."

CHAPTER 14

Max

MY WORDS CAME OUT MORE serious than I wanted them to, something that Aylin immediately caught onto.

Of course she would. She caught onto everything.

Instead of yelling at me for treating her like my possession or something just as equally fucked up, she grabbed a hold of my suit jacket and pinned me against the wall. She kissed me hard, her body pressing flush against mine as she did so.

God damn, she could actually knock the wind out of me if she really wanted to.

Before things got too out of hand, I cupped her jaw and tugged her away from me, giving me just enough room to look around the hall and spot a door that didn't seem to have a lock on it across the way from us.

Keeping my hand still cupped around her jaw, I walked her back until I had her pinned against it. Our kiss was heated and sloppy—all kinds of nasty that you'd find in that hot-ass sex that made you think about it for days.

I was so ready for my dick to be buried inside of her the moment I got this damn door open, even with my hands getting preoccupied with other things.

Aylin was gripping the front of my suit jacket again, already trying to get it off me while we were out in the open like this. It made me feel better that I wasn't the only one letting my more animalistic instincts take over the smarter part of my brain that was more than likely flashing a big red sign that said "DANGER" that I was completely neglecting to consider.

I really didn't care that hooking up with Aylin at an auction like this would most likely end in me getting stabbed or something else by my boss. All I cared about right now was me and here—the rest of the world could go fuck itself.

Finally, I managed to get my hand around the door handle and push the thing open. Both of us went tumbling backward and only with my quick reactions did it keep us from completely face-planting onto the floor.

Aylin snorted softly at me, pulling away just enough to look around the room—which turned out to be a supply closet—to search for a light of some sort. She grabbed a string hanging from the ceiling and tugged on it. A small bulb above us flickered to life.

"Nice," I said, swinging the door behind us shut.

Turned out there wasn't even a lock on the inside. What kind of jacked-up place was this that they allowed the public free access to their cleaning supplies?

Idiots.

Before I knew it, Aylin's hands were grabbing onto the front of my pants in order to tug at the belt. She pulled it from its loop and then from around my waist, causing me to raise my brows at her.

"You're not actually going to try and tie me up *again*, are you?"

She smiled at me. "What, didn't like it the first time?"

Uh... that wasn't exactly what I meant. One of these times I'd like to actually be able to touch her the whole time.

Before I could really argue with her, though, she pressed her body against me again. She swayed her hips against mine, teasing me with what little friction she was offering. It was both infuriating and erotic.

I felt a hand wrap around one of my wrists and bring it around behind me. Using my belt, she cinched both of my hands together behind my back, leaving me completely defenseless against whatever it was she had in mind for all of this.

I held in a sigh.

Well, hopefully she'll let me break out of these—

My train of thought completely derailed the second I noticed her slowly getting down onto her knees in front of me. My lips parted in surprise, keenly aware of every little twitch and tug of her fingers over my pants as she pulled them apart and then down just enough to expose me.

I was hard as fuck already, but seeing her down on her knees like this with my cock out resting right by her mouth was already making me want to come. I swallowed thickly, trying to hold it together before I did just that and force this to be over before it even started.

"See," she said, wrapping a hand around the base of me and stroked upward. "If you behave, you get rewarded."

A shudder worked its way up my spine at her words. Who knew I was into praise this much?

"Oh..." was all that I managed to say as my brain short-circuited completely.

I barely felt my head knocking back against the door the moment those sinful lips of hers wrapped themselves around the head of my cock. They created a suction that felt both incredibly euphoric and not enough all at once.

This skin at my wrists felt rough as I tugged at the restraints.

Desperately, I wanted to get out of it, to be able to thread my fingers through her hair and shove her head all the way down onto my cock until she choked and gagged on it. Until I could see her throat bob while it accommodated the intrusive size of me. I wanted to see the whites of her eyes as they rolled back into her head as she struggled.

Fuuuuck, I was going to cum just thinking about it.

I let out a pathetic moan.

She laughed around me, her tongue teasing the underside of me with a few careful swipes. "Who knew it was so easy to unravel a man like you, Graves?"

Fuck if I knew. Honestly, it was probably just the way I was about her. She drove me actually insane. She was like a worm that had embedded itself into my brain and was now piloting my body without my permission.

My hips jerked into her mouth, anticipating that wet heat wrapping farther down around me while I grew impatient. I knew she liked teasing me, but even just the few seconds this had been going on was enough to make me actually want to do something stupid.

But I waited. I behaved.

She popped her mouth off of me with a wet *pop* and then stroked her spit down the length of me. "You're being so good for me. Who knew you had it in you?"

My thighs shook slightly.

She's killing me.

Aylin wrapped her lips back around the head of my cock and then slid me deeper into her mouth. I forced my eyes open, having no idea when the hell they closed, in order to watch her as she hollowed out her cheeks.

She bobbed a few times, getting me nice and slick

while her other hand reached into my pants to cup my balls. She moved them around in her hands, rolling them at the same time that her mouth was moving on me.

I swore I'd had plenty of blowjobs before, but nothing had made me feel quite like a damn teenager than this right here, right now.

What the hell was happening to me?

"Oh fuck," I mumbled, my voice sounding strained.

My balls tightened, already ready to spill cum right onto that pretty little tongue of hers.

"Aylin..."

She looked up at me.

I let out a shuddering breath. "Touch yourself."

I refused to be the only one getting off right now. No way. I wasn't letting her walk out of this damn closet without at least an orgasm under her belt.

Her lips tightened around my cock, and surprisingly, she did as she was told. She paused moving her head and instead took her hand out from my pants and reaches down to where her slit rid up her thigh. She parted the fabric, revealing a thin piece of fabric that was just barely covering that incredible pussy of hers.

Her fingers moved slowly under the band of her panties, the outlined shape of them erotic as they moved around to part her lips. She groaned when she finally touched herself. Those pretty eyelashes of hers fluttered.

I watched in raptured attention as those fingers

moved under the thin fabric, rolling over her clit in slow circles.

"Fuck…" I breathed out.

She lapped at the head of my cock, catching all of the precum leaking out of it. It mixed with the spit already in her mouth, creating a frothy mixture that looked extra hot as she swallowed it.

A small groan left her lips when her fingers hooked again and plunged into her. Over and over she drew them back out, only to sink them in as deep as they could go. I could tell her pussy was wet from the sounds of her fingers kissing the edges of her hole with each pass.

Aylin looked up at me again, staring me down and then pulled me back into her mouth. She bobbed her head, faster than before. Both of us were in a race to get to our orgasms before the other could. My eyes flitted between her mouth on me and her fingers moving inside her, my attention ripped between both displays until it was too much for me to take. I came with a quick jerk of my hips and a short shout that had me banging my head back against the door again.

"Ohhhh fuck…!" I hissed, my cum spilling out of me in tight pulls.

I felt Aylin's mouth constrict around me, holding me in place as I coated the inside of her mouth and tongue. She groaned softly in what I hoped was her reaching her own orgasm judging by the sounds.

I panted slightly, giving myself a few seconds to breathe before I was leaning forward again to look at the mess of my date. She pulled her mouth off of me, swallowing everything that was inside of it, and then slowly took her hand out from under her panties.

My mouth watered at the sight of those glossy fingers.

"May I?" I asked.

She smiled and stood slowly, letting go of my cock, which flopped down uselessly, spent and still slightly tender feeling. Aylin held her fingers up to my mouth, just brushing them over my bottom lip. I caught both of them between my teeth and then wrapped my lips around them to suck.

I couldn't help but groan at the taste.

Damn, next time we did this, I needed to taste her for real.

Before I could really savor anything, though, Aylin pulled them out of my mouth before stepping back and saying, "I want to see the product that your boss has before it's on stage."

I blinked slowly at her. "Uhhh, what?"

She sighed at me. "Get me to Ricard Machiavelli, Max."

I'm sorry... what the hell is happening now? My sex-drunk mind wasn't exactly processing things clearly right now.

"Ayli—"

She fixed me with a hard look, pulling her dress back in place as she straightened herself up.

Okay, not the time to argue, I see.

I sighed. So long for post-sex glow. "All right... I can get you to him. But I can't promise you anything."

I reached around behind me to tug the belt off of my wrists. "Let me worry about that."

Weirdly enough, I didn't doubt her. She was a smart cookie, so whatever she was planning had to be good.

Damn, I was kind of sad this was over already. I was only just getting started.

Sighing again—to myself, mostly—I tucked all of my parts back into my pants and re-tucked my shirt. I grabbed my belt when she offered it to me and looped it back around my waist.

When we were finally all ready, we snuck out of the supply closet. I looked around the empty hall before grabbing onto her arm and tugging her along. Thankfully, in the time it took us to do our business, no one else had come wandering down this way.

We only needed one person to see us tangled up together and our whole plan would come completely unraveled.

As soon as we stepped back into the main hall, I let go of Aylin's arm and fixed my posture to look just as stuffy as the rest of the men in here.

I made my way back into the ballroom, passing by a group of associates that I noticed immediately eyed Aylin as we passed by. For some reason, them checking her out made me want to whip around and deck them all for daring to. Stupid, of course. She was hot, and anyone with a pair of eyes knew that.

Not to mention, it wasn't like we were *together* together.

But I doubted any of those men could handle a woman like her. Not like I could. She needed someone that could keep up with her, not a man that was too scared to even make a move.

Aylin was close to my side as we entered into the large room.

I spotted Ricard and his father over by the stage still and took the straight shot to them. While his father was engrossed in some kind of conversation, Ricard had his arms crossed over his chest as a deep frown was settled onto his face. Whatever the men around him were talking about, he clearly wasn't approving.

That... didn't forebode well.

The man to the right of Ricard was the first to lock eyes on us, breaking away from the conversation with Senior in order to say, "I didn't know we were allowed to bring dates."

Senior whipped around, his eyes narrowing at me before flitting to Aylin.

She stuck her hand out, pushing past me in order to present herself to Senior. "I'm actually here representing the Rosetti family. Don Rosetti sends his best wishes."

Ricard's brow shot us as he gave me a silent "*what the fuck?*" look. I gave him a subtle shrug in return.

Senior grasped Aylin's hand in his own, blinking slowly at her while taking her all in. I was sure having a woman here as beautiful as Aylin was not only surprising but intriguing too. She was a viper that could easily wind her way through a crowd, lulling people into a false sense of security with her beauty and quick tongue.

Hell, if I hadn't met her previously, I probably would be just as susceptible.

Actually, who was I kidding? I still was.

"Rosetti..." Senior spoke slowly. "Out in Chicago?"

She nodded, dropping her hand from his. "That's the one. He's interested in seeing the product ahead of the auction."

Around us, two of the men laughed.

Senior gave her a slow smile, one that suggested Aylin's words were not only stupid but naive as well. "It's an auction. The whole point is to—"

She didn't even let him finish before she was pulling her clutch out from under her arm and popping it open. She fisted a thick wad of cash that was rolled up into a tight bind and held it up to flash it at him.

"A hundred grand for a private viewing. Five minutes." She gave him a slow smile. "Per Don Rosetti's request."

Senior's eyes widened and then immediately snapped to the cash in her hand. He was practically salivating over it like a fucking drug addict.

"Five minutes, you say..." He trailed off, reaching for the bundle.

She snatched it back from him. "Five minutes. Uninterrupted. My boss wants to know if the product is worth his time."

One of the men behind Senior snorted. "Don Machiavelli has good product. You can trust his judgment in procuring it."

She ignored him, continuing to stare Senior down.

Next to her, I shifted slightly. Damn, if this was the kind of tactics that the Rosetti family used in order to get what they wanted, then Ricard and I definitely needed to look into getting on their good side. Because if Aylin was this much of a hurricane, I couldn't imagine what Gioni would be like when he wasn't being an absolutely unhinged brat.

"Five minutes," Senior said firmly, nodding. "Follow me."

CHAPTER 15

Aylin

My blood boiled the second the door was swung shut behind me, sealing me inside of the makeshift vault that stored all of the valuables that were to be auctioned off tonight.

Even after getting off like I did, it wasn't enough to calm me down in the slightest. Max was usually such a good distraction, but not this time around.

Max loitered by the door, giving me room to wander around uninhibited. He'd volunteered himself after I'd parted ways with my hundred grand and was led back here by Don Ricard, Sr. himself. The man had been apprehensive to leave me alone with everything, giving Max the perfect in to sneak himself in with me.

How far he was involved with this family, I still wasn't sure. It was hard to tell with him in general where his loyalties lay. Which made it all the more difficult to figure out what his actual motives were. Obviously, he and the younger Machiavelli were planning something, which I doubted the elder was aware of.

With the nature of how this entire situation was playing out and Max's insistence that he had no part in it, he seemed strangely protective of the heir as well.

I'd have to keep that in mind—given that it could be a point of contention if Max ever happened to piss me off again.

The thought *almost* made me smile. Honestly, I had no doubt he would. As much charm as he had, he was also skilled in being infuriating. Though that could also be because of my attractive for him was slowly starting to get out of hand.

I hadn't missed the way he looked me over once he'd spotted me outside of the ballroom. In fact, I'd had half a mind to drag him into an empty room to get him down on his knees for me and show me how sexy he *actually* found me. However, that would all have to wait. So long as my guns were being held hostage, I needed to stay vigilant.

Handing over a stack of cash to Don Machiavelli had pissed me off more than anyone could tell, but it was all a means to an end in the end. I'd get my money back and then some once I secured my shit. My revenge had been a slow boil ever since I'd gotten word of them yanking my shit.

Eventually, it was going to boil over and cause some chaos.

The cache of guns was stored toward the back of the room and caught my attention immediately.

Heading over to it, I could tell from here that it was indeed my supply, even without having to check the serial numbers. Simply by the sheer volume of what I'd been exchanging, this matched the shipment almost entirely.

It was a shame I didn't have time to catalog every single gun to make sure they were all accounted for, but if one or two of them had been pilfered off the top, then that gave me all the more reason to take it out on the Machiavellis once I had everything safe and sound back in Chicago.

"That all look familiar to you?" Max asked, still over by the door.

I took the time I had to glance around the room again. None of this shit was of any value to me, but that didn't have the means to take it with me after I had my shit secured. I was never interested in the trading of other goods such as fine jewelry, drugs, exotic animals, or even the occasional designer knockoffs.

None of that stuff, aside from drugs, would get you the kind of money I was used to bringing in. However, that didn't mean it wouldn't make for a good side hustle.

"Max," I said without turning around.

"Yeah?"

"When's the auction start?"

"Eight sharp. Why?"

I nodded, turning around slowly while taking my clutch out from under my arm. Popping it open, I grabbed my phone and flipped through my contacts until I landed on Dante's, sending over a quick text for the "go-ahead" signal.

"If I were you, I'd get out of here," I told him.

"Uh, what?"

Glancing up from my phone, I found myself wondering why in the world I was warning him ahead of time.

Did I... care if he got caught in the crossfire? I certainly never would've thought I did. Yet here I was, warning him to get himself and that Machiavelli brat out of here before my men rained down the hellfire I so wanted to wage the second I stepped foot in this god-forsaken desert.

"I'm not repeating myself."

His eyes narrowed slowly. "You're not... you..." He shook his head. "Aylin, you can't actually think you're going to be able to take all of this before the auction. There are like three dozen guards here just manning the doors."

"And? What's your point."

"My point is that that would be the dumbest suicide mission I've ever seen. And trust me, I've been on my fair share of them."

Interesting.

Every little piece he'd shown me of his past only teased me into wanting to know more. I hated that I wanted to, though. None of that information was useful to me. It gave me a sense of losing control—as if I somehow wanted him to stick around.

How annoying.

Maybe I should just let him die in the crossfires. At least then I wouldn't be worried about my head getting all sorts of tangled while he invaded my space.

"I'm not asking for your opinion on the matter," I said, snapping my clutch closed. "Take my warning or don't. I don't care."

Even as the words left my mouth, there was a bitterness to them. I didn't care—I really didn't. But then again...

No.

I didn't care.

I had better things to worry about than a man like him being foolish.

"Look," he stepped away from the door, coming closer to me, "just listen to me for a second. Don't try and have your guys bust through the doors while the event is going on. For one, you're going to bring a lot more attention to the Rosettis in a way that I'm sure your boss really wouldn't like."

The implication practically made my eye twitch. Even if my brother was *technically* the Don of our family, my entire syndicate knew that I was the one running the show. He was simply a convenient puppet-head.

Normally, people speaking like this never bothered me. It made me feel like I was getting away with a dirty secret that only I was privy to. However, Max thinking differently rubbed me the wrong way. I wanted him to see me for the woman that I was—the one running the show and calling the shots. The woman behind the mask that was pulling the strings and creating all of these decisions in the first place.

It was so stupid. So, so stupid for me to be even *tempted* to tell him. Why the fuck should I care about his approval? I didn't. *I don't.*

I hated that it still bothered me.

He wouldn't find me half as attractive if he knew the real me. That much I was sure of.

The thought helped me reel myself back from biting into him and showing him that dark side of me that was boiling just under the surface of my patience.

"Two," he went on. "It'll be better if you take your shit *after* the show's over."

"I'm not waiting that long."

He sighed at me. "Aylin, please. If you and your boss want any kind of contact with these people in the future, whether that be for deals or exploiting them, I don't know, you need to think about this rationally. I know it's frustrating to know that all your shit is here and someone's going to bid on it and try to sweep it out from under you. But that doesn't mean you need to sit back and let that happen."

"I'm not *paying* for what's already mine, Graves," I snapped.

"That's not what I'm saying." He was close enough to me now that he could reach out and grab me. His voice was soft as he spoke. "I'm saying that you take it when they're least expecting it."

I stared at him for a long moment, trying to figure out just what the fuck he meant.

Those gray eyes of his watched me expectantly. Like he knew I'd figure it out once I thought about it for a minute. There was a small smile playing on his lips that I doubted he realized he was showing. When the fuck did he become so attached to me that he was giving me advice? When the fuck did I become reasonable enough with him that I was actually listening?

"After they're loading it," I said slowly. "That's when we'd strike."

He grinned, nodding. "Think about it. They'll have just enough guys to load everything into whoever's vans are taking it. All of these big wigs are going to be too busy celebrating with each other to notice their guys being picked off in the parking lot."

He had a point. A good one at that.

Damn. I really hated that I was considering this and not going with my original plan to practically mow down anything that moved in order to get to what I wanted.

I sighed.

"I'll help you," he offered immediately.

I rolled my eyes. "I don't need your help. I'm perfectly capable of doing this myself."

"I know you are. But let me help anyway. I know the ins and outs of the Machiavellis. Since he's running the show, there's bound to be drinks pouring soon. Tell your guys to hold off and wait. I can give you the heads-up when everything's being loaded out the back after the show. It'll be way easier for me to sneak around than you looking like that."

I raised a brow. "Oh? And what's that supposed to mean?"

His grin turned devilish. "You know *exactly* what it means. Don't play coy with me."

I couldn't help but mirror his expression. I did.

In fact, getting dressed today, I'd had him in mind. I'd wanted to tantalize him enough to make it almost unbearable that he couldn't have me. That was my favorite part about all of this. I liked watching him practically get on his knees and beg for me like a fucking dog.

Rolling my shoulders back, I pulled my phone back out of my bag and sent a quick text over to Dante. His answer was rather immediate, giving me the "all clear" that our men were on standby for the time being.

I let out a slow breath.

If all of this went according to plan, I'd have my weapons and my men all ready to head back to Chicago tonight, leaving this damn city and desert behind for good.

I tried not to really look too deeply into the way my heart panged uncomfortably at the thought of this being my last night with Max. It had to be this way. He was way too big of a distraction for me to take him with me. Plus, I didn't have time to unravel where his loyalties were, and I wasn't about to have a mole among my ranks.

"I'll let you know when things are winding down," he said, winking at me.

My heart panged again.

Fuck.

"Keep me updated. I'll be waiting," I said before heading over to the door and giving it a solid knock to be let out.

CHAPTER 16

Aylin

As Max wandered off, I took the time to mingle with a few of the other patrons in order to not only blend in, but to see who else was interested in my cache.

It turned out, there were quite a few that had specifically come here for the amount of weapons that had been rumored to be up for sale—a fact that had my eye twitching at the thought of someone else manhandling my property.

No matter how much my shit sold for, I knew I'd be getting it back. The only question was how many bodies would I need to drop in order to do so.

I wasn't worried about any of the cleanup after the fact. Dante was already on it, handling whatever needed to be taken care of once we were good to go and on our way back to Chicago. I was putting a lot of faith in his abilities to handle this—something that I normally wouldn't ever have to question. But given the fact that he'd been bootlicking my brother as of late and coddling him to no end, it was making me second guess everything on the table.

Speaking of which...

I should check up on that brat.

Excusing myself from the small group of men that had gathered around me, I stepped out of the ballroom, vaguely hearing the auctioneer call to everyone that the first sale would be starting in a few minutes.

Guests around me all started to file into the ballroom, giving me enough privacy to find myself a corner of the parlor to hide myself in while I called my brother.

He picked up on the fourth ring. "What?"

I crossed one of my arms over my chest, hooking my hand in the crook of my elbow. "What are you doing?"

He scoffed. "The fuck're you talking about? I just got up."

I shifted my arm slightly, checking the thin 14k gold bracelet on my wrist that doubled as a small watch. "It's almost midnight over there."

"Okay, and? I had a long night yesterday."

I gritted my teeth to keep myself from laying into him and gathering unwanted attention my way. "Where's Frankie?"

"I don't know. Why are you calling me to ask?"

Because he's supposed to be watching you, was what I wanted to spit out. Dante was Gioni's typical day-to-day watchdog, but with him being here in Nevada with me, I'd asked Frankie to take over the role instead.

I got that my brother was hard to handle when I wasn't around, but what the fuck was I paying these people for if they couldn't control him while I was off doing more important things?

This was only furthering my need for a complete restructure of our entire network. I was tired of chasing people down and hounding them about doing their damn jobs.

"Gioni," I growled. "Have you seen Frankie since I left?"

"Yeah. He's been up my ass. I bet you told him to do that. You know, I don't need a babysitter."

"I don't care what you want. You're to behave while I'm not there. If I come home and find out you've done something stupid, you're going to regret ever stepping out of line."

He scoffed again. "What are you doing to do, lock me in the basement like Mom used to?"

"You're going to wish that's the only thing I'll do to you. Don't threaten me with your bad attitude. You think you can play this game with me? I'll show you who's really in charge."

He was quiet for a long moment, my words sinking in slowly. Gioni, as much of an outspoken brat as he was, had never been stupid. He knew when he royally pissed me off and that I wasn't one to make empty threats. If I was promising him a punishment, then I damn well meant every word of it.

"You want to talk to him, then call him," he finally said. "Last I saw of him was last night at dinner. That's it."

"And what's been going on while I've been away?"

"Nothing."

"Gioni."

"Aylin," he countered. "I haven't done anything. You want to blame me for whatever fuck up is going on, then let me tell you something. It's not on me. That's on you. So fix your own shit and stop trying to pass the blame around."

While I doubted Frankie had told him the real reason I was out here, it wouldn't surprise me if my brother already had suspicions. Again, he wasn't stupid. Unfortunately. If he was, he would be ten times easier to control and not the goddamn loose cannon I was sadly stuck with.

"I'm coming home tonight," I told him.

He sighed at me. "Fine. There's a meeting with another buyer tomorrow morning."

Perfect timing.

"Make sure you're up for it," I told him. "I'm not going to be nice if I have to have Dante drag you out of bed."

"Whatever," he said and then dropped the call on the other line.

Honestly, what I wouldn't give to ship him off overseas.

A thought occurred to me. Actually... that wasn't half a bad idea. I had a strong connection over there to a family in Ireland that would probably be able to slap a few good manners into my brother that my method clearly wasn't achieving.

After I was back in Chicago, I'd have to give Amelia a call. It would be nice to catch up with her and check in on how things were over there.

My phone vibrated in my hand, alerting me to an incoming text. Max's name scrolled across my screen.

Auction's started. Yours up first, it read.

I backed out of the thread and shoved my phone back inside of my clutch.

Showtime.

As it turned out, my entire cache of weapons sold for just under two million dollars.

I was hardly shocked by how much the price had been driven up by a few of the more rambunctious buyers. Not only were they military-grade, but they were the real deal. No knock-offs or off-brands in sight. I only dealt with high-quality product, and that showed with how much my shit went for at market.

I'd kept a close eye on Don Machiavelli the entire time the bidding had been going on. He'd practically salivated as the price had continued to go up, his face becoming flushed from the amount of money he was about to come into.

That was interesting to me. I hadn't heard anything about their financial status, but it was clear to me that either Ricard Sr. was simply money-hungry or had some financial strains happening behind the scenes by this kind of outward reaction.

It would certainly make sense as to why he'd been dumb enough to steal from me and then turn around immediately and sell it.

After all of this was said and done, perhaps I'd think about getting the real truth from Max. I was sure he'd be more than happy to give me the low-down, even if it meant giving his enemy trade secrets.

Not only that, but it would give me a prime opportunity to test how brittle his leash of loyalty was to that family.

I really need to stop thinking about kidnapping him.

Even if the thought was incredibly tempting the longer I sat here with my bidding fan surrounded by money-hungry vagrants, watching them spend a disgusting amount of money.

In any case, I'd have my hands full with my brother once I got home.

Either way, I had much to do after all of this.

Once the auction was finally concluded and the last item—a mid-century collection of pottery stolen from a famous gallery—had been auctioned off, patrons began to get up from their seats and head to a set of doors that opened up on the side of the ballroom to another room that looked like it had been set up for cocktails.

I stayed in my seat, fanning myself with my bidding fan. I hadn't seen Max since before my phone call with my brother, and even now, as people were starting to leave the auction, I still couldn't spot him in the crowd.

Where my clutch was resting on my lap, I could feel my phone vibrating inside of it. Pulling it out, I looked at the screen to see a text from none other than the man himself.

Guns being loaded up. Three vans belonging to Reynolds family. Want their plates?

I blinked down at my screen. Not even five minutes after the entire event had ended, my shit was already being taken for transport. Jesus, was Machiavelli eager to get his cash and split?

I texted him back, *Tail them. I'll track your location and send my men after you.*

He responded immediately. *Kinky ;)*

I rolled my eyes. He was lucky I didn't have a set of handcuffs on me or else I'd be tying him up to a fucking streetlamp before leaving on my way to the airport.

Getting out of the text thread and to the one I had with Dante, I filled him in on the details, waiting for the confirmation of my message being received before pocketing my phone and standing up.

Now. Time to get this fucking over with.

CHAPTER 17

Max

RICARD and I loitered at the fringes of the loading dock, keeping ourselves in the shadows while we watched Aylin's supply of guns get loaded up.

Honestly, I wasn't shocked that they were already starting to move it. A cash cow like that needed to be kept locked up properly, or you ran the risk of getting completely annihilated like the cartel had been.

Not to mention, there had been a lot of interest from a couple of parties. So I was sure the Reynoldses wanted to get a fucking move on before anyone got any wise ideas.

That was the risk you ran while running in these types of circles, though. Everyone had self-interests that were never going to align with your own. You needed to figure that shit out quick or you were going to end up losing everything you ever managed to scrape up by the skin of your teeth while climbing your way to the top.

I held my phone tight in my hands, checking the screen for a text from Aylin even though I knew she was most likely not going to reply to me. She was more than likely busy with her boss, talking to him about their next steps.

It had been interesting to me to see her thinking through my proposition to her in the vault. I really wished I knew what was going on in that head of hers while she was running through whatever scenarios that were keeping her from speaking out loud to me.

If only she had the proper opportunities to shine, she really would be such a hurricane of a woman dominating these kinds of spaces without being held back by someone like Gioni or his inner circle. I could tell as I talked with her that she'd had very little restraint in refuting me about her working for a man like him.

I could tell she agreed and she wanted to outwardly say it as fact. Both of us knew that she was much too good to be in the position she'd found herself in. And that wasn't just me saying this because I found her attractive and would probably do anything in my power to get her back into bed with me.

Outside of all of that, she truly was every inch the viper she portrayed herself as.

It's too bad she couldn't run her own syndicate. And even if she had the backing for it, it wasn't like she wouldn't be able to be out in the open. She'd need to do it in the shadows, and that wasn't any place for a woman like her to be. She needed to be out on the front lines, taking down those that stood in her way and smiling when they saw her face as the one to pull the trigger.

A shame, really. All of it.

"Hey." I felt Ricard nudge me. "They're getting ready to leave."

The second the words left his mouth, the last of the guns had been handed over and placed inside of the last van, the door swinging shut and locked right behind.

I straightened up and pulled up my text thread with Aylin, filling her in on the details. We waited for the crew to head back in through the side door leading into the venue before coming out from the shadows and hopping down onto the loading dock.

There was no one else out here, other than us and the three vans that had Aylin's cache in them. The first one, in the front, took off first, pulling out and around to the front of the venue to head out onto the main street. The second and third both started their engines, heading off after it.

"We're following them, right?" Ricard asked, jogging over to a car we'd stashed before the auctions had started in order to make our getaway quick.

I nodded to him, getting into the driver's seat and starting the car the second Ricard had his feet tucked inside the cab. He slammed the door shut, not bothering to buckle before we were speeding off after the three vans.

"You think they're going to stay local?" he asked

me, readjusting himself in order to grab his gun out from where he'd tucked it into his belt.

"They might. If they were smart, they'd get out of state tonight," I said, glancing in the rearview for anyone following us as we pulled out onto the main street.

I had no clue how Aylin was going to be tracking me, but I assumed she had some way of getting into my phone and following the GPS. Honestly, I didn't really care how she figured it out—so long as we got her her shit back, that was fine with me.

I wanted her to go back home to Chicago happy, not be stuck here for another few weeks trying to track down where the Reynoldses kept their stashes.

Or even worse—trying to find the shit on the black market.

That would be a fucking nightmare trying to pry it away from gangs' hands in order to turn around and re-sell it. If worse came to worse, though, I was sure Aylin wouldn't mind calling her boss up and having him send down a few groups of associates to tag-team a gang's hideout.

We were kind of one in the same, with the only stark difference between a mafia family and a street gang being notoriety and established dominance within city limits.

And also public influence—that went a long way too.

We followed after the vans for just a little over fifteen

minutes until the streets opened up into more residential areas, giving me a foreboding feeling. While it wasn't uncommon for families to hide in plain sight, this was a strange location to be taking in order to get to a safehouse.

Would it be my first time being at a safehouse in the middle of a neighborhood that looked like it was straight out of a ritzy magazine inside of a doctor's office?

Well, yes actually.

"Where the fuck are we going?" Ricard verbalized my internal thoughts, clearly having the same as me.

"Don't know."

"Trap?"

"Don't know," I answered again, glancing in the rearview once more.

There was another car that was now trailing behind us. I hoped like fuck it was one of Aylin's because if not, we were walking into a damn landmine field.

We didn't stop at all as we made our way through the neighborhood and instead took a right that led us down a dead-end road that looked run down and much less taken care of. All three vans stopped in front of a dilapidated-looking house, two of the drivers getting out of the vehicles in order to come around and pop open the backs of their trunks.

Hm, storing that kind of product in a place like this.

Well, I supposed there was a first for everything.

I parked us a ways down from where they were,

killing the lights on my car before we could be spotted. The car in back of me pulled around to head toward the house, stopping about two car lengths away from where the drive of the house started.

That was odd—

Just then, four other cars made their way down the dead end, all of them coming around to block the street at odd angles. Men poured out of the cars, all racing toward the vans and the men that were in the middle of unloading the cache.

"Oh fuck," I mumbled, kicking my door open and getting out.

Just as Ricard was doing the same, that's when the bullets started flying.

"Shit!" I ducked around to the other side of the car, grabbing Ricard as he did the same and keeping him practically down on the ground.

"In the middle of a fucking street?!" he hissed. "What kind of assholes do they think—"

He was cut off by the sound of screeching tires. I popped my head up over the trunk of our car, seeing headlights coming right toward us.

Oh fuck!

Ripping Ricard up from the ground, I threw him into the grass next to the street. He tucked and rolled, giving me just enough space to dive on after him. The sound of one of the cars smashing directly into our own was not only loud, but startling.

Tires screeched loudly as the car—van, now that I could turn and look at it—forced its way through from being pinned against what was left of the front of the car we'd taken here.

"Up!" Ricard shouted at me, getting up onto his feet and whipping his gun out to shoot two guys that were running toward us.

I gritted my teeth, following after him.

At the house, I could see that there were still two vans left parked in front of it.

By the time the third van had gotten through and was now careening down the street away from the scene, I had my gun out and poised in front of me. Another man came around from one of the sides of the first van and started to shoot at us.

I body-checked Ricard back away from it, pushing him toward a set of bushes that had definitely seen better days. The sound of a bullet zinging by my ear had me pulling my trigger in a knee-jerk reaction.

Fuck, we needed to get the hell out of here.

I glance over at our car. Totaled.

Fuck.

A car screeched to a halt next to us, the window already rolled down as a woman—Aylin—leaned out of it. She had a gun in her hand, expertly held and aimed at the man by the van. Before I could even blink, blood splattered everywhere against the side of the van, the man's head whipping back to slam against it as he slid down onto the ground unmoving.

My eyes widened.

Holy hell.

"Get in the car!" she yelled before leaning back in.

Damn, what a woman.

I grabbed onto Ricard's arm and dragged him along with me. After shoving him into the backseat, I climbed into the passenger's side, my heart pounding in my chest as she slammed her foot down onto the floor and took off even before we both had our doors closed.

There was a determined set to her face that I couldn't help to stare at, taken in by the sheer blood-thirsty nature of what had just happened and simultaneously not surprised at all that she had it in her.

Holy fuck, I wanted her so bad.

"Hold on," she said, both hands clutching the steering wheel tight.

And hold on I fucking did.

CHAPTER 18

Aylin

I JERKED THE WHEEL AROUND, sending both men inside of the car careening against their windows as we sped through the streets of downtown Vegas.

"Damn!" the Machiavelli brat spat out. "Learn how to fucking drive!"

I ignored him, flooring the gas and running through another redlight. Horns blared around us, none of which were cop lights flashing at me, so I didn't care to pay attention to them.

Next to me, Max grunted and pushed himself up. His gun was clutched tight in his hand, the safety already pulled back and ready to use. I took another sharp turn after the van in front of me, not letting them get even a few feet from my field of view.

If these fuckers wanted a car chase, than that's what they were going to get.

We pulled off on one of the side streets, racing through a residential area until we came up to another intersection. The van blew through the light, nearly clipping a truck on the way through. I paused with my foot jamming down on the brakes, looking quickly both ways before punching it again.

"Max," I barked out. "My phone. Check my texts."

"Right now?!" he asked even though he was already pivoting in his seat to grab my clutch that I'd thrown onto the floor in the back.

"I need to know Dante got the other two vans secured."

He grunted at me, halfway wedged between the two front seats. I heard the sound of my clutch popping open before he was pushing himself back into his seat.

"Dante you said?"

"Yes." I reached over to press my thumb against the screen, unlocking it for him.

He looked down at it, scrolling for a few seconds before saying, "He says they're secured. All wrapped up. Just loading them in a moving van."

Excellent. Only one more to go.

By the time all of this was done, I needed a fucking drink.

And a good lay.

Preferably both.

One thing at a time, though.

The van's lights flared up ahead before disappearing down another side street that I soon followed after. The second I had my hands on these fucking guys, they were going to wish they'd never decided to leave the damn scene.

Glancing in the rearview, I could see that we had another car coming up on our ass and fast. Whoever it was had clearly been sent to shake us off.

Pulling my eyes back to the road, I noticed that within another second, the van's lights shut off, shrouding it in complete darkness as it entered into an unmarked industrial park. A chain-link fence snapped as the van blew through it, giving me enough visibility to follow after them before I couldn't see anything else at all.

I rolled down my window again, listening for the sounds of screeching tires as they came to a halt up ahead.

Bingo.

I jammed on my own brakes, torquing the wheel and spinning us around hard enough to slam the back end of the car into the other one that had been tailing us.

Max was the first to react, leaning his upper body out his window and firing a few rounds at the front windshield. Both men jolted back as the glass shattered, ducking down in order to avoid the spray.

I kicked my door open while hiking up the skirts of my dress in order to tie them up at my hip, leaving my legs free to move around in. It wasn't ideal to run in heels, but I'd done so with worse circumstances.

Grabbing my gun, I left my door open and jogged toward where I'd last heard the van. There was no light back here, but I could hear the sounds of guns going off behind me as Max and Junior finished off our tail.

I had half a mind to stay and make sure they were good, but I trusted Max had it handled. He'd be a poor excuse of an ex-ops soldier if he wasn't.

I spotted the van up ahead, looking completely abandoned as I got closer to it. Ducking around the side of it, I held my gun up and worked my way around to the front.

No one in the front seat.

Sound caught my attention, a door slamming near me as someone headed into the building.

I followed after them, leaving the van for Max to find.

As much as I wanted to grab my shit and go, I needed to make sure whoever the fuck this was didn't get any slick idea on trying to come back around to shoot us when we were busy loading everything up into my own van.

Inside of the building, the hallway smelled old and sour. There was only one light that barely worked—an old exit sign by the looks of it—covered in dust and other grime that made it hard to see as I traveled down the long hallway.

There was another door at the end of it, already pushed wide open and flowing into a larger room that looked like an old factory.

Across the way, I saw two figures trying to make their way quietly through the mess that had been left behind by whoever it was that owned this place before it went under. One of them tripped, causing them both to falter in their steps.

"Don't move," I told them, pointing my gun at the one that was still standing.

They both froze at the sound of my gun clicking.

My heels were loud as I walked toward them, their arms up while the one standing slowly turned to face me. He was wearing a nicely tailored suit—not something I would've guessed for an associate to own judging by how nicely it was pressed.

His salt-and-pepper hair complimented the dark suit while a pair of gold-rimmed glasses were resting on the bridge of his nose.

My finger flexed on the trigger. It didn't look like either of them had any weapons on them. Which would make sense as to why they'd been running instead of trying to mow us down.

"Don't," the other man hissed at the one still on the dirty floor when he tried to move.

I couldn't see his face, as he was turned away from me. But the second he tried to get up, I pulled back the trigger, firing off my gun and hitting the man right in the back of the head. His body jerked forward, folding in on itself before flopping down onto the ground motionless.

The man who'd been standing took off, running quicker than I was expecting for a man his age.

A loud noise behind me had me pivoting on my feet, turning just in time to avoid a bullet flying my way. I ducked behind a large industrial-looking machine, giving me enough cover to avoid being shot in the back as I made my way away from the main part of the factory floor.

A small group of men that I recognized as the ones that had been hanging around Don Reynolds came running inside, all of them with their guns facing out in front of them.

I found a spot that was far enough away and gave me enough cover in the darkness before I fired off two rounds, getting the one closest to me in the leg and side of his chest.

He screamed and went down, alerting the others into firing at me.

I ran through to another machine, crouching down as I listened to the sounds of bullets hitting against metal.

Fuck, Max better hurry up.

Just as the thought filtered in through my mind, I heard another pained grunt and the sound of a body dropping close to where the men had been standing.

"Fuck!" one of them said. "Spread out—"

He was cut off suddenly, a gurgling sound choking him out.

"Left!" Max yelled, presumably to his companion.

Another gun went off.

I grinned.

Right on fucking time.

CHAPTER 19

Ricard

I PANTED, my gun slightly wavering in my hand as the dust settled and the sounds of bullets ricocheting off of the walls around us finally silenced.

There was nothing else other than the sound of my own breathing that reached my ears.

Fuck, was everyone else dead?

Next to me, movement caught my eye, causing me to whip around with my gun brandished. Max's own gun met mine—both of us relaxing at the same time.

"Fuck," I mumbled, lowering mine.

He sighed, shaking off the adrenaline. "We need to find Aylin."

"Over here," she called, somewhere toward the back of the building from where we'd first come in.

The sound of her heels clicking on the cement floor had us both turning toward it. She appeared out of what looked like thin air, her red dress a beacon in the poor lighting.

Max was the first to start moving, heading over to her as she made her way through the carnage and over to a lone body that was laying away from the rest of ones we'd taken down.

Bodies were littered all over the floor, blood pooling around them in a weirdly artistic-macabre sort of way that made me think of those stupid-ass paintings that had been getting auctioned off only a few hours ago.

What had surprised me the most wasn't the fact that more backup had shone up just as the gun fight had started, but it was at how easily it seemed we'd been able to blow through them all.

For a mafia family like the Reynoldses, it seemed weird to me that they had such untrained men working for them.

We stumbled upon Aylin, who was bent over one of the bodies of the backup that had rushed in. She was crouched down, looking at the man whose face was pressed down onto the cement floor while a bullet hole shown wet in the back of his head.

She was frowning down at the man, looking him over while she patted the side of his pants pocket.

"What's up?" Max asked her, hovering closer to her than he should've been.

"Seems odd. I don't recognize him."

I popped a brow. "Okay and? You know every associate that works for each family?"

She looked over her shoulder at me, narrowing her eyes. "He isn't an associate."

"How do you know?" Max asked before I could.

She pulled her hand out of his pocket, brandishing an ID. "Because he was at the auction."

Max slipped it from her fingers, turning it over to see the front of it.

"I recognized him when he came in," she went on. "I thought it was odd, so I followed him over here and shot him before he could escape."

Max was still staring down at the ID, his lips parted in what looked like surprise. "What... the..."

I reached over to grab it from him, narrowly missing as he sidestepped me to move over to where Aylin was. He squatted, grabbing the back of the man's suit jacket in order to roll him over onto his back so that his face was sunny-side up.

What shocked me wasn't the fact that the guy was in fact one of the people that had been at the auction, but that he was someone I recognized and knew.

"What the fuck is your cousin doing here, Ricard?" Max turned to look at me.

I stared down in abject shock as Antoni's slack face and glazed-over eyes greeted me.

What... the fuck..?

"He works for you?" Aylin asked, looking between us.

"He's..." I could barely get the words out. What the fuck was going on? "He's my father's cousin. My second cousin. I... Why's he here?"

Aylin stood slowly. "He's clearly been double-crossing you if he's working for the Reynoldses."

Max shook his head. "No way. He's loyal to Senior. Always has been."

"Clearly not," she argued back.

I cleared my throat, trying to force my thoughts together. "You think my father sent him here to get the guns back?"

Max shook his head again. "Why would he? He's already got the money. That's all he cared about."

That made sense. But why the fuck would Antoni be here then? As Max said, he was loyal to a fault for my father. Neither he nor his brother would ever step out on the family in order to... work with some other one that barely had any recognition outside of this city.

That was too small of a pond to go jumping into from the lake he'd been swimming in previously.

"He..." I swiped a hand over my brow. "Maybe he got spooked with all the financial stuff back at home. He could've been trying to get insider secrets to sell back to my father."

"Can't see that happening," Max countered again. "He would've had better luck trying to get in with the Rosettis."

True...

Then what—?

"You're having financial problems." Aylin fixed me with a hard look. "Right?"

I hesitated before saying, "Not me specifically."

"Your father, though. That's why he stole all my shit."

"There's been a..." Max squinted. "Bit of a turnover problem lately."

Aylin nodded. "Seems to me that whatever is going on, there was a motive of money behind it. It could be something as simple as a double pay day. Or like you were saying, selling info. Either way, you're both in deep shit."

"Why?" I frowned.

The fuck, was she actually going to try to exploit my family's financial situation now of all times? After we just got her fucking guns back for her?

I glared over at Max, who blinked at me innocently.

I swear to fucking god...

"Well, I didn't get both of them," she said.

Max and I stared at her.

"Both of who?" he asked.

She nodded down to my cousin. "Both of them. He has a twin, right? Least that's what it looked like when I saw them both shooting at me."

My mouth dropped open.

Oh fuck.

Ohhhhhh fuck.

No. No way.

They were both here?

Holy fuck, my father was actually going to kill me.

"Shit," Max mumbled.

Aylin had the audacity to laugh. "I guess that means you'll both be looking to cash in a favor?"

I glared at her, my temper suddenly flaring. "Fuck you. You think you can just take advantage of this situation? We just saved your ass. You know that, right?"

Max held up a hand to me. "Aylin."

She crossed her arms over her chest, smirking at him. "You need a place to lay low, right?"

"What are you suggesting exactly?"

Her smirk widened. "You'll be coming with me to Chicago. Since what he said was true and you did in fact save my ass, I suppose that means you get to cash in a favor. I'll house you until you can get right with whatever it is you two are planning behind Don Machiavelli's back."

Max let out a choked sound, probably surprised she'd even called him out like that. I wasn't, though. She was a fucking snake and probably had figured we were stepping out on my dad long before any of this chaos started. I was sure Gioni had been filling her head with it the second we'd left their estate to come back to Vegas.

She wasn't wrong, obviously. But fuck if he wasn't making us look absolutely transparent as fuck.

I opened my mouth to tell her to fuck right off with that offer but caught Max's side-eye before the words could come out of my mouth.

I knew exactly what that look meant.

We were going to be going to fucking Chicago.

"Thank you, Aylin," he said. "Thank you for helping us."

She practically preened. "You're welcome. Now let's get going. The plane leaves in an hour."

Fuck.

Fuck me sideways and fuck me till fucking Sunday.

Before You Go...

If you enjoyed my book please take a second to leave a short review. These reviews help me as an author to be found by other amazing readers like you.

Thank you so much! :)

About the Author

Simone Fox is a steamy romance author who loves to write about sexy bad boys.

When she's not working on her next book, she's traveling or hanging out with family.

Keep up with all things Provoked here ➔ https://www.facebook.com/groups/simone.fox